A CAVALCADE OF GOBLINS

A CAVALCADE OF

GOBLINS

EDITED BY
ALAN GARNER

ILLUSTRATED BY
KRYSTYNA TURSKA

NEW YORK
HENRY Z. WALCK, INCORPORATED

First published in Great Britain 1969
as *The Hamish Hamilton Book of Goblins*

© 1969 ALAN GARNER

Illustrations © 1969 KRYSTYNA TURSKA

Standard Book Number: 8098–2407–8

Library of Congress Catalog Card Number: 69–17905

PRINTED IN GREAT BRITAIN

Prayer

Graunt that no Hobgoblins fright me,
No hungrie devils rise up and bite me;
No Urchins, Elves, or drunkards Ghoasts
Shove me against walles or postes.
O graunt I may no black thing touch.
Though many men love to meet such.

JOHN DAY

Contents

Introduction

WE have always tried to make sense of the natural forces in the world and of the hidden forces in ourselves. Sometimes we give them shapes as gods and devils: sometimes we subject them to rules, which we call magic. This book tries to show a little of our fear and our wonder.

It is a personal selection. For example, certain qualities of imagination speak more clearly to me than others do, and so there are several British, Japanese and North American Indian legends here, and none at all from Greece and Rome. Classical myth leaves me as cold as its marble.

A man could write in England three hundred years ago: "Our mothers maids have so terrified us with an ouglie divell having hornes on his head, fier in his mouth, and a taile in his breache, eies like a bason, fanges like a dog, claws like a beare, and a voice roring like a lion, whereby we start and are afraid when we hear one cry Bough; and they have so fraied us with bull beggers, spirits, witches, urchens, elves, hags, fairies, satyrs, pans, faunes, sylens, kit with the cansticke, tritons, centaures, dwarfes, giants, imps, calcars, conjurers, nymphes, changlings, Incubus, Robin good-fellowe, the spoorne, the mare, the man in the oke, the hell waine, the fierdrake, the puckle, Tom thombe, hob gobblin, Tom tumbler, boneles, and such other bugs, that we are afraid of our own shadows."

Little has changed since then. We have lost our faith in the terror of the corn field and the dark wood, but we still need terror. Boneles and such other bugs now ride flying saucers, and it is in the nearest galaxy, not the churchyard, that menace lies. Goblins are mere-steppers, boundary-haunters; and there will always be boundaries.

A.G.

Gobbleknoll

THERE was a hill that ate people. The Rabbit's grandmother told him never to go near it.

So the Rabbit went to the hill, and shouted, "Gobbleknoll, swallow me! Come, devour me!"

But Gobbleknoll knew the Rabbit, and took no notice.

Later that day, a group of travellers came by, looking for a place to shelter from the rain, and Gobbleknoll opened his green and ferny lips, and the travellers thought that they had found a cave. They went in, and the Rabbit slipped close behind them. But the hill felt hairy pads on his tunnels, and before the Rabbit could reach the middle, Gobbleknoll threw him out, and the grass shut.

The Rabbit went and hid behind a tree, and a few days later a hunting party arrived at the hill just before night, and Gobbleknoll opened again. This time the Rabbit used magic art, and took the shape of a man, except for his ears, which he tucked down his shirt, so that they would not brush against the roof and make Gobbleknoll sneeze.

He went down long and horrid passages, until he came to the hill's stomach, and there were the remains of all the victims, and some who were not yet dead.

"Hey hey hey!" shouted the Rabbit. "Why don't you eat? You leave the best! Here's a delicious heart. What's wrong with that?"

Gobbleknoll set up a dismal howling, for it was his own heart that the Rabbit had seen. And the Rabbit knew this,

and took out a knife, and stabbed the hill dead. The ground split, and the blue sky lit the deep hollows, and the living came out and wept before the Rabbit, and wanted to give him power and riches. But all the Rabbit would take was Gobbleknoll's fat, and he went home with it on his back, and he and his grandmother were fit to burst from it for many a day.

John Connu Rider

When John Connu come', he come' wit' style
An' wit' plenty noise an' plenty practice
From way back 'cross plantation lawn
An' 'ill-an'-gully rider.

John Connu got 'orse-'ead an' 'ouse-top
An' king-'ead an' bird-body
An' 'nough other t'ings that frighten
Mos' o' we, bad.

John Connu sing' an' John Connu dance'
An' Connu walk' 'ard
An' Connu walk' sof'
An' Connu' eye got eyewater in it
When he laugh'.

ANDREW SALKEY

Vukub-Cakix

HUN-APU and Xbalanque were twin hero-wizards, warriors and mischief-makers, both the pride and the torment of Guatemala.

Vukub-Cakix, the Great Macaw, was nothing but trouble. He shone with the brilliance of gold and silver, and his teeth were emeralds, and he owned the nanze-tree of succulent fruit. He was a boaster, and his sons were no better. Their names were Zipacna the Earthmaker and Cabrakan the Earthshaker. The sons made mountains and then toppled them, and the father guzzled the harvests, so that between them they were a plague in Guatemala.

One day Vukub-Cakix climbed his nanze-tree to eat the fruit, but the fruit had been eaten already. He swung in the tree-top, screaming his rage, but the rage turned to pain as a blow-pipe dart struck him on the jaw, and he lost his grip and tumbled to the ground. While he lay there, winded, Hun-Apu jumped on him out of a bush and began to strangle him. Vukub-Cakix would have died then if he had not seen the pulp of the nanze-fruit smeared round Hun-Apu's mouth. This angered Vukub-Cakix more than his throttling, and he swelled into monster-fury and tore Hun-Apu's arm from its shoulder.

Vukub-Cakix went home with the arm, still chattering vengeance, and he built a fire and put the arm on a spit to roast. Then he lay on his bed in a sulk and nursed his jaw.

Hun-Apu found his brother Xbalanque. "We must get

my arm back," he said, "before it's cooked, or it will be stiff for life." So they made their way as doctors to Vukub-Cakix's house.

"We are famous doctors," they said, "and from the noise we hear there must be somebody in need of us."

"Aiee," said Vukub-Cakix. "Aiee."

"That sound I diagnose as a bad case of Grimgums," said Xbalanque.

"Og, og," moaned Vukub-Cakix.

"And that's Eyetitis," said Hun-Apu.

"They'll have to come out," said Xbalanque.

"Yes, all out," said Hun-Apu.

"But shall I be cured?" said Vukub-Cakix.

"Cured?" said the twins. "Why, you'll not recognize yourself."

So they took out Vukub-Cakix's teeth and put in grains of maize, but they gave him nothing for his eyes. And from that moment Vukub-Cakix was harmless. His colours faded, his mouth was no terror, and whether or not he died, or wandered in the forest as a beggar, no one knew or cared. Hun-Apu pulled his arm off the fire and stuck it back on his shoulder.

But the twins had not yet finished their work. Vukub's two sons were still alive, and trouble enough without the need to avenge their father's disaster. They decided to deal with Zipacna the Earthmaker first, and got four hundred young men to help them.

The young men pretended to be building a house. They cut down the biggest tree of Guatemala, and Zipacna found them heaving and straining to lift it.

"Oh, Sir," they said, "please help us carry this tree. It is the ridge of our new house, which we are making as an offering to those two heroes, the sons of Vukub-Cakix."

"Weaklings," said Zipacna, and hefted the tree on to his shoulder.

"This way," said the four hundred young men. "This way, if you please, Sir."

The giant carried the tree through the forest to a clearing where the young men had dug a pit deeper even than the giant was tall.

"That is for the foundations, Sir," they said. "Would you be so good as to take the tree down there?"

Zipacna jumped into the pit. "Foundations are a funny place for roof ridges, aren't they?" he said. In answer, the

young men piled logs and rocks on his head, and when the pit was a mound, they danced on it to celebrate the death of Zipacna.

But Zipacna was not dead. He was holding his strength, and when he felt that all the young men were above him on the mound, he burst upwards, the great mountain-maker, and his force sent the young men flying into the sky, where they have remained ever since as the Pleiades, waiting for someone to help them down.

Hun-Apu and Xbalanque had watched all this, and felt that they now had the measure of their enemy.

They made a ravine below a mountain range, and at the bottom of the ravine they carved an enormous crab out of stone, and painted it so that it seemed alive. Crabs were Zipacna's favourite food. Then the twins spread the rumour that the biggest crab in the world was hiding in the ravine, and before long Zipacna came to investigate. When he saw the crab he swallowed it at a gulp.

"Good," he said. "But heavy. No doubt I'll be sorry."

And he was. The twins diverted a river into the ravine, and Zipacna was too weighted to swim, and the twins pushed the whole range on top of him and shaped it into a single mountain over his head, so that Zipacna was both drowned and buried, and he lies under Mount Meahuan even now.

This left Cabrakan the Earthshaker.

The twins worked on him through his conceit.

They found Cabrakan throwing rocks about. He took no care for anything. If one flattened a village, it was just too bad.

"Good morning," said Hun-Apu. "Would you tell us what you are doing?"

"Can't you see?" said Cabrakan.

He lobbed a boulder into a maize crop.

"And who are you two?"

"We have no names," said the twins. "We hunt with the blow-pipe, and since we never meet anyone, we need no names. But may we stay and watch you?"

"If you like," said Cabrakan.

The twins sat and stared at Cabrakan with the unwinking eyes of children, and said nothing, nor showed themselves impressed by anything he did. Cabrakan tried all the harder to make these two hunters applaud, until after a week of mountain-hurling he was dizzy with hunger and fatigue.

Hun-Apu then shot a bird and baked it in clay for the giant, but the clay he used was poisoned, and when Cabrakan took up his work again he trembled as if with fever.

"Our father was a weak man," said Xbalanque, "but he did all you have done. His favourite game was to throw that mountain over there into the sea."

Cabrakan strove to focus his eyes through the sweat.

"What, that little white pimple of quartz?" he said. "That's too small for me to bother with."

"So you say," said Hun-Apu.

"And so I'll show," said Cabrakan. He staggered to the hill and put his arms about it.

Now this hill was not like any other hill or mountain. It had no roots in the earth, but was a piece of the earth itself that showed through the land, an unbroken, shining rock that went on for ever beneath the giant's feet.

So Cabrakan, exhausted by his efforts, poisoned by his enemies, took hold of the world and tried to lift it. His knees knocked like war-drums.

"We've been wasting our time," said Xbalanque.

"I knew he couldn't," said Hun-Apu.

Cabrakan gave one great heave. The top of his head blew off. And that was the last of the race of Vukub-Cakix in Guatemala.

Tops or Bottoms

Brownie was a type of goblin that lived in and around the farmhouse. He would often work for the people on the farm, but he had an unpredictable temper, and sometimes, as in this story, he was much more trouble than he was worth.

THERE was a brownie once who got above himself, and thought that because he stacked the hay (if he felt like it), and cleaned up in the kitchen (if it wasn't too mucky), the whole farm belonged to him. He was for giving the farmer marching orders.

Of course farmer will have none of that, so brownie makes a great to-do at night, and it's half a day's work regular to clear up after him around the house. Well, then farmer gives over leaving milk out in a saucer by the hearth; and so it goes from bad to worse.

Anyway, brownie must have the big field, he says, and they chunner and chunner, calling each other all the names, so as women have to cover their ears for language. Anyway, it's left that farmer will do the work, and they'll share the crop half and half between them.

When Spring comes, farmer says, "Which will you have, tops or bottoms?"

"Bottoms," says brownie.

So farmer plants wheat, keeps the grain for himself, and gives brownie the roots and stubble.

Next year, farmer says to brownie, "Which will you have, tops or bottoms?"

"Tops," says brownie.

So farmer plants turnips, and brownie is left to make what he can of the leaves.

He'll have none of it the next year: not tops or bottoms: he will not. Corn, says brownie, that's what it must be, and the field divided in half, and brownie and farmer to have a mowing match, winner keep all.

July next, farmer goes to the blacksmith and has ever so many thin iron rods made, and he plants them all over brownie's half of the field.

Anyway, they start mowing at daybreak. Farmer walks through his patch, up and down, sweet as a comb, but brownie's snagged like I don't know what.

"Mortal hard docks, these: mortal hard docks," he keeps clacking.

Anyway, after an hour of this the rods have knocked the edge from his scythe and it's as blunt as a plough handle, and brownie is right borsant.

Now in a match, mowers take time off together for sharpening up; so brownie calls to farmer, "When do we wiffle-waffle, mate?"

"Oh, about noon, maybe," says farmer.

"Noon!" says brownie. "I've lost my land!"

He drops his scythe, and he's never seen on that farm again. And no wonder.

The Voyage of Maelduin

Adapted from the Translation of KUNO MEYER

I have to admit to a weakness for Celtic legends. It would be all too easy to fill this book with them. For me, no other people were so rich and terrifying in their imagination. They found no need to explain: the stories often appear to be strung together at random—and yet there is always the feeling that everything is very simple. We are looking at a real and brilliant and logical world through strange glass.

You can take this story all at once, or bit by bit. All at once will crowd your brain with colour: bit by bit will make thoughts like yeast.

The Voyage of Maelduin's Boat This. Three Years and Seven Months Was It Wandering in the Ocean.

THERE was a famous man of the Eoganacht of Ninuss (that is, the Eoganacht of the Arans): his name was Ailill of the Edge of Battle. A mighty soldier was he, and a hero-lord of his own tribe and kindred. And there was a young nun, the prioress of a church of nuns, with whom he met. Between them both there was a noble boy; Maelduin, son of Ailill, was he.

Now this boy was reared by the king's queen, and she gave out that she was his mother.

Now the one fostermother reared him and the king's three sons, in one cradle, and on one breast, and on one lap.

Beautiful indeed was his form, and it is doubtful if there

13

has been in flesh anyone as beautiful as he. So he grew up till he was a young warrior and fit to use weapons. Great, then, was his brightness and his gaiety and his playfulness. In his play he outwent all his comrades, both in throwing balls, and running, and leaping, and putting stones, and racing horses. He had truly the victory in each of those games.

One day, then, a certain haughty warrior grew envious against him, and he said in raging anger, "You," he said, "whose clan and kindred no one knows, whose mother and father no one knows, to vanquish us in every game, whether we contend with you on land or on water, or on the draughtboard!"

So then Maelduin was silent, for till that time he had thought that he was the son of the king and of the queen his fostermother. Then he said to his fostermother, "I will not eat and I will not drink until you tell me," said he, "my mother and my father."

"But," said she, "why are you asking after that? Do not take to heart the words of the proud warriors. I am your mother," said she. "The love of the people of the earth for their sons is no greater than the love I bear to you."

"That may be," said he: "nevertheless, make known my parents to me."

So his fostermother went with him, and delivered him into his mother's hand; and thereafter he entreated his mother to declare his father to him.

"Silly," said she, "is what you are doing, for if you should know your father you would have no good of him, and you will not be the gladder, for he died long ago."

"It is the better for me to know it," said he, "however it be."

Then his mother told him the truth. "Ailill of the Edge

of Battle was your father," said she, "of the Eoganacht of Ninuss."

Then Maelduin went to his fatherland and to his heritage, having his three fosterbrothers with him; and beloved warriors were they. And then his kindred welcomed him, and gave great courage there.

At a certain time afterwards there was a number of warriors in the graveyard of Dubcluain, putting stones. So Maelduin's foot was planted on the scorched ruin, and over it he was flinging the stone. A certain poison-tongued man—Briccne was his name—said to Maelduin: "It were better," said he, "to avenge the man who was burnt there than to cast stones over his bare burnt bones."

"Who was that?" said Maelduin.

"Ailill," said he, "your own father."

"Who killed him?" asked Maelduin.

Briccne replied: "Raiders of Leix," said he, "and they destroyed him on this spot."

Then Maelduin threw away the stone which he was about to cast, and took his mantle round him, and his armour on him; and he was mournful. And he asked the way to go to Leix, and the guides told him that he could go only by sea.

So he went into the country of Corcomroe to seek a charm and a blessing of a wizard who lived there, to begin building a boat. Nuca was the wizard's name, and it is from him that Boirenn Nuca is called. He told Maelduin the day on which he should begin the boat, and the number of the crew that should go in her, which was seventeen men, or sixty according to others. And he told him that no number greater or less than that should go; and he told him the day he should set to sea.

Then Maelduin built a three-skinned boat; and they

who were to go in it in his company were ready. German was there and Diuran the Rhymer.

So then he went to sea on the day that the wizard had told him to set out. When they had gone a little from land, after hoisting the sail, then came into the harbour after them his three fosterbrothers, the three sons of his foster-father and fostermother; and they shouted to them to come back again to them to the end that they might go with them.

"Get you home," said Maelduin; "for even though we should return to land, only the number we have here shall go with me."

"We will go after you into the sea and be drowned there, unless you come to us."

Then the three of them cast themselves into the sea, and they swam far from land. When Maelduin saw that, he turned towards them so that they might not be drowned, and he brought them into the boat.

I

They rowed that day till evening, and the night after it till midnight, when they found two small bald islands, with two forts in them; and then they heard out of the forts the noise and outcry of the drunkenness, and the soldiers, and the trophies. And this is what one man said to the other: "Stay off from me," said he, "for I am a better hero than you, for it is I that slew Ailill of the Edge of Battle, and burnt Dubcluain on him; and no evil has so far been done to me by his kindred for it; and you have never done the like of that!"

"We have the victory in our hands!" said German, and

said Diuran the Rhymer. "Let us go and wreck these two forts."

As they were saying these words, a great wind came upon them, so that they were driven over the sea all that night until morning. And even after morning they saw neither earth nor land, and they knew not where they were going. Then said Maelduin: "Leave the boat still, without rowing."

Then they entered the great, endless ocean; and Maelduin afterwards said to his fosterbrothers: "You have caused this to us, hurling yourselves upon us in the boat in spite of the words of the enchanter and wizard, who told us that on board the boat we should go only the number that we were before you came."

They had no answer, save only to be in their little silence.

2

Three days and three nights were they, and they found neither land nor ground. Then on the morning of the third day they heard a sound from the north-east. "This is the voice of a wave against a shore," said Maelduin. Now when the day was bright they made towards land. As they were casting lots to see which of them should go on shore, there came a great swarm of ants, each of them the size of a foal, down to the strand towards them, and into the sea. What the ants desired was to eat the crew and their boat: so the sailors fled for three days and three nights; and they saw neither land nor ground.

3

On the morning of the third day they heard the sound of a wave against a beach, and with the daylight they saw an island high and great; and banks of earth all round about it. Lower was each of them than the other, and there was a row of trees around it, and many great birds on these

trees. And they were taking counsel as to who should go to explore the island and see whether the birds were gentle. "I will go," said Maelduin. So Maelduin went, and warily searched the island, and found nothing evil there. And they ate their fill of the birds, and brought some of them on board their boat.

4

Three days and three nights were they at sea after that. But on the morning of the fourth day they saw another great island. Sandy was its soil. When they came to the shore of the island they saw there a beast like a horse. The legs of a hound he had, with rough, sharp nails; and huge

was his joy at seeing them. And he was prancing before them, for he longed to devour them and their boat. "He is not sorry to meet us," said Maelduin; "let us go back from the island." That was done; and when the beast saw them fleeing, he went down to the strand and began digging up the beach with his sharp nails, and pelting them with the pebbles, and they did not expect to escape from him.

5

When they went from the island they were a long while voyaging, without food, hungrily, till they found another island, with a great cliff round it on every side, and therein was a long, narrow wood, and great was its length and its narrowness. When Maelduin reached that wood he took from it a rod in his hand as he passed it. Three days and

three nights the rod remained in his hand, while the boat was under sail, coasting the cliff, and on the third day he found a cluster of three apples at the end of the rod. For forty nights each of these apples fed them.

6

Then afterwards they found another island, with a fence of stone around it. When they drew near it a huge beast sprang up in the island, and raced round about the island. To Maelduin it seemed swifter than the wind. And then it went to the height of the island, and there it performed the trick known as "straightening of body", that is, its head below and its feet above; and so it continued; it turned in its skin, that is, the flesh and bones revolved, but the skin outside was unmoved. Or at another time the skin outside turned like a mill, the bones and the flesh unmoved.

When it had been doing this for a long while, it sprang

up again and raced about the island, as it had done at first. Then it returned to the same place; and that time the lower half of its skin stayed still, and the other half above ran round and round like a millstone. That, then, was its practice when it was going round the island.

Maelduin and his people fled with all their might, and the beast saw them fleeing, and it went into the beach to seize them, and began to hit them with stones of the harbour. Now one of these stones came into their boat, and pierced through Maelduin's shield, and lodged in the keel of the boat.

7

Now their hunger and thirst were great, and when their noses were full of the stench of the sea they sighted an island which was not large, and therein a fort surrounded by a white, high rampart as if it were built of burnt lime, or as if it were all one rock of chalk. Great was the height from the sea: it all but reached the clouds.

The fort was open wide. Round the ramparts were great, snow-white houses. When the warriors entered the largest of these they saw no one there, save a small cat which was in the midst of the house, playing on the four stone pillars that were there. It was leaping from each

pillar to the other. It looked a little at the men, and did not stop itself from its play. After that they saw three rows on the wall of the house round about, from one doorpost to the other. A row there, first, of brooches of gold and of silver, with their pins in the wall, and a row of neck-torques of gold and of silver; like hoops of a vat was each of them. The third row was of great swords, with hilts of gold and of silver.

The rooms were full of white quilts and shining garments. A roasted ox, moreover, and a flitch in the midst of the house, and great vessels with good intoxicating drink.

"Has this been left for us?" said Maelduin to the cat. It looked at him suddenly, and began to play again. Then Maelduin recognized that it was for them that the dinner had been left. So they dined and drank and slept. They put the leavings of the drink into the pots, and stored up the leavings of the food.

Now when they proposed to go, Maelduin's third
fosterbrother said: "Shall I take with me a necklace of these
necklaces?"

"No," said Maelduin. "Not without a guard is this
house."

Howbeit the fosterbrother took it as far as the middle of
the enclosure. The cat followed them, and leapt through
him like a fiery arrow, and burnt him so that he became
ashes, and went back till it was on its pillar.

Then Maelduin soothed the cat with words, and set the
necklace in its place, and cleansed the ashes from the floor
of the enclosure, and cast them on the shore of the sea.

Then they went on board their boat.

8

Early on the morning of the third day after that they
espied another island, with a brazen palisade over the
midst of it which divided the island into two, and they
espied great flocks of sheep therein, a black flock on this
side of the fence and a white flock on the far side. And they
saw a big man separating the flocks. When he used to

fling a white sheep over the fence from this side to the black sheep it became black at once. So, when he used to cast a black sheep over the fence to the far side, it became white at once. The men were adread at seeing that.

"This were well for us to do," said Maelduin. "Let us cast two rods into the island. If they change colour, we shall change if we land on it."

So they flung a rod with black bark on the side where were the white sheep, and it became white at once. Then they flung a peeled, white rod on the side where were the black sheep, and it became black at once.

"Not encouraging was that experiment," said Maelduin. "Let us not land on the island. Doubtless our colour would have fared no better than the rods."

They went back from the island in terror.

9

On the third day afterwards they saw another island, great and wide, and a great mountain in the island, and they proposed to go and view the island from it. Now when Diuran the Rhymer and German went to visit the mountain they found before them a broad river which was not deep. Into this river German dipped the handle of his spear, and at once it was consumed, as if fire had burnt it. And they went no further.

10

They found a large island, and a great multitude of human beings therein. Black were these, both in bodies and raiment. Bands round their heads, and they rested not from wailing.

An unlucky lot fell to one of Maelduin's two foster-brothers to land on the island. When he went to the people who were wailing he at once became a comrade of theirs, and began to weep along with them. Two were sent to bring him back, and they did not recognize him amongst the others, and they themselves turned to lament.

Then said Maelduin, "Let four go," said he, "with your weapons, and bring you the men by force, and look not at the land nor the air, and put your garments round your noses and round your mouths, and breathe not the air of the land, and take not your eyes off your own men."

The four went, and brought back with them by force the other two, but not the fosterbrother. When they were asked what they had seen in the land, they would say, "Indeed, we know not; but what we saw others doing, we did."

Thereafter they came rapidly from the island.

II

Thereafter they came to another lofty island, wherein were four fences, which divided it into four parts. A fence of gold, first: another of silver: the third of brass: and the fourth of crystal. Kings in the fourth division, queens in another, warriors in another, maidens in the other. A

maiden went to meet them, and brought them on land, and gave them food. They likened it to cheese; and whatever taste was pleasing to anyone he would find it there. And she poured to them out of a little vessel, so that they slept a drunkenness of three days and three nights. All this time the maiden was tending them. When they awoke on the third day they were in their boat on sea. Nowhere did they find their island or their maiden.

Then they rowed away.

12

They heard in the north-east a great cry and chant. That night and the next day they were rowing that they might know what cry or what chant they heard. They beheld a high, mountainous island, full of birds, black and dun and speckled, shouting and speaking loudly.

13

They rowed a little from that island, and found another island that was not large. There were many trees, and on them many birds. And after that they saw in the island a man whose clothing was his hair. So they asked him who he was, and from where his kindred.

"Of the men of Ireland am I," said he. "I went on my pilgrimage in a small boat, and when I had gone a little from land my boat split under me. I went again to land," said he, "and I put under my feet a sod from my country, and on it I got me up to the sea. And that sod is established here for me in this place, and a foot is added to its breadth each year from that time to this, and a tree every year to grow therein. You shall all," said he, "reach your country save one man."

14

After that they voyaged till they entered a sea that resembled green glass. Such was its purity that the gravel and the sand of the sea were clearly visible through it; and they saw no monsters nor beasts therein among the crags, but only the pure gravel and the green sand. For a long space of the day they were voyaging in that sea, and great was its splendour and its beauty.

15

They afterwards put forth into another sea like a cloud, and it seemed to them that it would not support them or the boat. Then they beheld under the sea down below them roofed strongholds and a beautiful country. And they saw a beast huge, awful, monstrous, in a tree there, and a drove of herds and flocks round about the tree, and beside the tree an armed man, with shield and spear and sword.

When he beheld yon huge beast that abode in the tree he went from there in flight immediately. The beast stretched forth its neck out of the tree, and set his head into the back of the largest ox of the herd, and dragged it into the tree and devoured it in the twinkling of an eye. The flocks and the herdsmen fled away at once; and when Maelduin and his people saw that, greater terror and fear seized them, for they supposed that they would never cross that sea without falling down through it, by reason of its tenuity like mist.

So after much danger, they passed over it.

16

Thereafter they found another island, and up around it rose the sea, making vast cliffs of water all about it. As the people of that country perceived them, they set to screaming at them, and saying, "It is they! It is they!" till they were out of breath.

Then Maelduin and his men beheld many human beings, and great herds of cattle, and troops of horses, and many flocks of sheep. Then there was a woman pelting them from below with large nuts which remained floating on the waves above them. Much of these nuts they gathered and took with them. They went back to the island, and thereat the screams ceased.

"Where are they now?" said the man who was coming after them at the scream.

"They have gone away," said another group of them.

"They are not so," said another group.

Now it is likely that there was someone concerning whom the islanders had a prophecy that he would ruin their country and expel them from their land.

17

They got them to another island, wherein a strange thing was shown to them, to wit, a great stream rose out of the island, and went, like a rainbow, over the whole island, and descended into the other strand of the island on the other side thereof. And they were going under the stream without being wet. And they were piercing with their spears the stream above; and great, enormous salmon were tumbling from above out of the stream down upon the soil of the island. And all the island was full of the stench of fish.

18

Thereafter they voyaged till they found a great silvern column. It had four sides, and the width of each of these sides was two oarstrokes of the boat, so that in its whole circumference there were eight oarstrokes of the boat. And not a single clod of earth was about it, but only the boundless ocean. And they saw not how its base was below, or—because of its height—how its summit was above. Out of its summit came a silvern net far away from it; and the boat went under sail through a mesh of that net. And Diuran gave a blow of the edge of his spear over the mesh.

"Destroy not the net," said Maelduin, "for what we see is the work of mighty men."

"I do this that my tidings may be the more believed," said Diuran.

And they heard a voice then from the summit of yonder pillar, mighty, and clear, and distinct. But they knew not the tongue it spoke, or the words it uttered.

19

Then they saw another island, standing on a single pedestal, to wit, one foot supporting it. And they rowed round it to seek a way into it, and they found no way thereinto; but they saw down in the base of the pedestal a closed door under lock. They understood that that was the way by which the island was entered. And they saw a plough on the top of the island; but they held speech with no one, and no one held speech with them. Then they went away back to sea.

20

They found a large island, with a great level plain therein. A great multitude was on that plain, playing and laughing without any cessation. Lots were cast by Maelduin and his men to see unto whom it should fall to enter the island and explore it. The lot fell to the first of Maelduin's fosterbrothers. When he went he at once began to play and laugh continually along with the islanders, as if he had been with them all his life. His comrades stayed for a long, long space expecting him, and he came not to them. So they left him.

21

After that they sighted another island, which was not large; and a fiery rampart was round it; and that rampart kept turning about the island. There was an open doorway in the side of that rampart. Now, whenever the doorway would come opposite to them, they would see through it the whole island, and all that was therein, and all its indwellers, even human beings, beautiful, abundant, wearing adorned garments, and feasting with golden vessels in their hands. And the wanderers heard their ale-music. And for a long space were they seeing the marvel they beheld, and they judged it delightful.

22

Now, after they had gone from there they came to an island with abundant cattle, and with oxen and kine and sheep. There were no houses nor forts therein, and so they ate the flesh of the sheep. Then said some of them, seeing a large falcon there, "The falcon is like the falcons of Ireland!"

"That is true, indeed," said some of the others.

"Watch," said Maelduin, "and see how the bird will go from us."

They saw that it flew from them to the south-east. So they rowed after the bird in the direction in which it had gone from them. At nightfall they saw land like the land of Ireland. They rowed towards it. They found a small island, and it was from this very island that the wind had snatched them into the ocean when they first went to sea.

Then they put their prow to the shore, and they went to the fortress that was in the island, and they were listening, and the inhabitants of the fortress were then dining.

They heard some of them saying, "It is well for us if we should not see Maelduin."

"That Maelduin has been drowned," said another man to them.

"Perhaps it is he who shall wake you from your sleep," said another.

"If he should come now, what should we do?"

"That is not hard to say," said the chief of the house. "Great welcome to him if he should come, for he has been a long time in trouble."

Thereat Maelduin struck the clapper against the door-valve.

"Who is there?" said the doorkeeper.

"Maelduin is here," said he himself.

"Then open!" said the chief. "Welcome is your coming."

So they entered the house, and great welcome was made to them, and new garments were given them.

Maelduin then went to his own district, and Diuran the Rhymer took the five half-ounces of silver he had brought from the net. And they declared their adventures from beginning to end, and all the dangers and perils they had found on sea and land.

Now Aed the Fair, chief sage of Ireland, arranged this story as it stands here; and he did it so for delighting the mind and for the people of Ireland after him.

The Fort of Rathangan

The fort over against the oak-wood,
Once it was Bruidge's, it was Cathal's,
It was Aed's, it was Ailill's,
It was Conaing's, it was Cuilne's,
And it was Maelduin's;
The fort remains after each in his turn—
And the kings asleep in the ground.

Translated by KUNO MEYER

Willow

IN a village there stood a green willow tree. For centuries the people loved it. In summer it was a place where villagers could meet after work and the heat of the day, and talk there till the moonlight fell through the branches. In winter it was a half-opened umbrella covered with snow.

A young farmer named Heitaro lived near the tree, and he, more than any other, loved the huge willow. It was the first thing he saw on waking, and the last at sleeping. Its shape greeted him when he returned from the fields, and all day he could see its crest. Sometimes he would burn a joss-stick beneath its branches and kneel down and pray.

One day an old man of the village came to Heitaro and explained to him that the people were anxious to build a bridge over the river, and that they particularly wanted the willow tree for timber.

"My dear willow for a bridge?" said Heitaro, covering his face. "Planks below feet? No! Take my own trees first, and spare the willow."

The villagers accepted Heitaro's trees, and the willow stood.

One night, while Heitaro was sitting under the tree he saw a beautiful woman close beside him. She stood, and looked at him shyly, as if she wanted to speak.

"Honourable lady," said Heitaro, "I shall go home. I see

you wait for somebody you love, and my presence here is uncouth."

"He will not come now," said the woman.

"Has he grown cold?" said Heitaro. "It is terrible when a mock love woos and leaves ashes."

"He has not grown cold," she said.

"And yet he does not come?" said Heitaro. "What strangeness is this?"

"He has come! His heart has been always here, here under this willow tree." And the woman smiled, and left him.

Night after night they met there. The woman's shyness disappeared, and it seemed that she could not hear too much praise of the willow tree from Heitaro's lips.

One night he said to her, "Little one, will you be my wife?"

"Yes," she said. "Call me Higo, and ask no questions, for love of me."

Heitaro and Higo were married, and they had a son called Chiyodo, and they were happy.

Great news came to the village, and it was not long before Heitaro learnt it. The Emperor wished to build a temple in Kyoto, and his ministers were searching the land for the best of timber. It would be an eternal honour to have given even a fragment of that holy shrine, and the villagers looked around them for a sacrifice that would be worthy.

There was only the willow.

Heitaro offered every tree on his land, and the price of his farm, but only the willow had the quality that was sought.

"Oh, wife, my Higo," he said that evening, "they are going to cut down the willow. Before I married you I could not have endured it. But, having you, perhaps I shall get over it some day."

The same night, Heitaro held his wife close for comfort in his sorrow, but he was woken by a loud cry.

"It grows dark!" said Higo. "The room is full of

whispers. Are you there, Heitaro? Listen! They are cutting the willow tree!"

"Hush, my love, hush. I am here."

"They are cutting me! Look how the shadow trembles in the moonlight! They are killing me! Oh, how they cut and tear! The pain, the pain! Put your hands here, and here. Surely the blows cannot fall now!"

Heitaro tried to ease her pain, but nothing he did could heal her.

"Love," she said, pressing her wet face to his, "I am going now. My body is breaking. Such a love cannot be cut down. Heitaro. Heitaro. My hair is falling through the sky!"

The willow tree lay green and tangled on the ground.

The Term

A rumpled sheet
of brown paper
about the length

and apparent bulk
of a man was
rolling with the

wind slowly over
and over in
the street as

a car drove down
upon it and
crushed it to

the ground. Unlike
a man it rose
again rolling

with the wind over
and over to be as
it was before.

WILLIAM CARLOS WILLIAMS

Edward Frank and the Friendly Cow

AS Edward Frank was coming home one night, he
heard something walking towards him, but at first
could see nothing. Suddenly his way was barred by
a tall, dismal object which stood in the path before him.

It was a marvellous-thin man, whose head was so high
that Edward nearly fell
over backward in his
efforts to gaze at it. His
knees knocked together,
and his heart sank. With
great difficulty he gasped
forth: "In the name of
God, what is here? Turn
out of my way, or I will
strike thee!"

The giant then dis-
appeared, and the fright-
ened Edward, seeing a
cow not far off, went
towards her to lean on
her, which the cow stood
still and permitted him
to do.

Yallery Brown

This story, and "The Green Mist", were told by the old people and the young children who lived in Lincolnshire before the fenlands were drained. I think that "Yallery Brown" is the most powerful of all English fairy tales.

I'VE heard tell as how the bogles and boggarts were main bad in the old times, but I can't rightly say as I ever saw any of them myself; not rightly bogles, that is, but I'll tell you about Yallery Brown. If he wasn't a boggart, he was main near it, and I knew him myself. So it's all true—strange and true I tell you.

I was working on the High Farm to then, and nobbut a lad of sixteen or maybe eighteen years; and my mother and folks dwelt down by the pond yonder, at the far end of the village.

I had the stables and such to see to, and the horses to help with, and odd jobs to do, and the work was hard, but the pay good. I reckon I was an idle scamp, for I couldn't abide hard work, and I looked forward all the week to Sundays, when I'd walk down home, and not go back till darklins.

By the green lane I could get to the farm in a matter of twenty minutes, but there used to be a path across the west field yonder, by the side of the spinney, and on past the fox cover and so to the ramper, and I used to go that way. It was longer for one thing, and I wasn't never in a hurry to get back to the work, and it was still and pleasant like of

Summer nights, out in the broad silent fields, mid the smell of the growing things.

Folk said as the spinney was haunted, and for sure I have seen lots of fairy stones and rings and that, along the grass edge; but I never saw nowt in the way of horrors and boggarts, let alone Yallery Brown, as I said before.

One Sunday, I was walking across the west field. It was a beautiful July night, warm and still, and the air was full of little sounds, as if the trees and grass were chattering to their selves. And all to once there came a bit ahead of me the pitifullest greetin I've ever heard, sob, sobbing, like a bairn spent with fear, and near heart-broken; breaking off into a moan, and then rising again in a long, whimpering wailing that made me feel sick nobbut to hark to it. I was always fond of babbies, too, and I began to look everywhere for the poor creature.

"Must be Sally Bratton's," I thought to myself. "She was always a flighty thing, and never looked after it. Like as not, she's flaunting about the lanes, and has clean forgot the babby."

But though I looked and looked I could find nowt. Nonetheless the sobbing was at my very ear, so tired like and sorrowful that I kept crying out, "Whisht, bairn, whisht! I'll take you back to your mother if you'll only hush your greetin."

But for all my looking I could find nowt. I keekit under the hedge by the spinney side, and I clumb over it, and I sought up and down by, and mid the trees, and through the long grass and weeds, but I only frightened some sleeping birds, and stinged my own hands with the nettles. I found nowt, and I fair gave up to last; so I stood there, scratching my head, and clean beat with it all. And presently the whimpering got louder and stronger in the

quietness, and I thought I could make out words of some
sort.

I harkened with all my ears, and the sorry thing was
saying all mixed up with sobbing:

"O, oh! The stone, the great big stone! O, oh! The stone
on top!"

Naturally I wondered where the stone might be, and I
looked again, and there by the hedge bottom was a great
flat stone, near buried in the mools, and hid in the cotted
grass and weeds. One of those stones as were used to call
the Strangers' Tables. The Strangers danced on them at
moonlight nights, and so they were never meddled with.
It's ill luck, you know, to cross the Tiddy People.

However, down I fell on my knee-bones by the stone,
and harkened again. Clearer nor ever, but tired and spent
with greetin came the little sobbing voice.

"Ooh! Ooh! The stone, the stone on top."

I was misliking to meddle with the thing, but I couldn't
stand the whimpering babby, and I tore like mad at the
stone, till I felt it lifting from the mools, and all to once it
came with a sigh, out of the damp earth and the tangled
grass and growing things. And there, in the hole, lay a
tiddy thing on its back, blinking up at the moon and at me.

It was no bigger than a year-old brat, but it had long
cotted hair and beard, twisted round and round its body,
so as I couldn't see its clouts. And the hair was all yaller and
shining and silky, like a bairn's; but the face of it was old,
and as if it were hundreds of years since it was young and
smooth. Just a heap of wrinkles, and two bright black eyes
in the mid, set in a lot of shining yaller hair; and the skin
was the colour of the fresh turned earth in the Spring—
brown as brown could be, and its bare hands and feet were
brown like the face of it.

The greetin had stopped, but the tears were standing on its cheek, and the tiddy thing looked mazed like in the moonshine and the night air. It was wondering what I'd do, but by and by it scrambled out of the hole, and stood looking about it, and at myself. It wasn't up to my knee, but it was the queerest creature I ever set eyes on. Brown and yaller all over; yaller and brown, as I told you before, and with such a glint in its eyes, and such a wizened face, that I felt feared on it, for all that it was so tiddy and old.

The creature's eyes got some used to the moonlight, and presently it looked up in my face as bold as ever was.

"Tom," it says, "you're a good lad."

As cool as you can think, it says, "Tom, you're a good lad," and its voice was soft and high and piping like a little bird twittering.

I touched my hat, and began to think what I had ought to say; but I was clemmed with fright, and I couldn't open my gob.

"Houts!" says the thing again. "You needn't be feared of me; you've done me a better turn than you know, my lad, and I'll do as much for you."

I couldn't speak yet, but I thought: "Lord! For sure it's a bogle!"

"No!" it says, quick as quick, "I'm not a bogle, but you'd best not ask me what I am; anyways, I'm a good friend of yours."

My very knee-bones struck, for certainly an ordinary body couldn't have known what I'd been thinking to myself, but it looked so kind like, and spoke so fair, that I made bold to get out, a bit quavery like:

"Might I be asking to know your honour's name?"

"Hm," it says, pulling its beard, "as for that," and it thought a bit, "ay so," it went on at last, "Yallery Brown you may call me; Yallery Brown. It's my nature, you see. And as for a name, it will do as well as any other. Yallery Brown, Tom, Yallery Brown's your friend, my lad."

"Thank you, master," says I, quite meek like.

"And now," he says, "I'm in a hurry tonight, but tell me quick, what shall I do for you? Will you have a wife? I can give you the rampingest lass in the town. Will you be rich? I'll give you gold as much as you can carry. Or will you have help with your work? Only say the word."

I scratched my head. "Well, as for a wife, I have no hankering after such. They're but bothersome bodies, and

I have women folk to home as will mend my clouts. And for gold; that's as may be," for, you see, I thought he was talking only, and may be he couldn't do as much as he said, "but for work—there, I can't abide work, and if you'll give me a helping hand in it, I'll thank you."

"Stop," says he, quick as lightning. "I'll help you, and welcome, but if ever you say that to me—if ever you thank me, do you see?—you'll never see me more. Mind that now. I want no thanks, I'll have no thanks, do you hear?" And he stamped his tiddy foot on the earth and looked as wicked as a raging bull.

"Mind that now, great lump as you be," he went on, calming down a bit, "and if ever you need help, or get into trouble, call on me and just say, 'Yallery Brown, come from the mools, I want thee!' and I shall be with you to once. And now," says he, picking up a dandelion puff, "good night to you." And he blowed it up, and it all came in my eyes and ears.

Soon as I could see again, the tiddy creature was gone, and but for the stone on end, and the hole at my feet, I'd have thought I'd been dreaming.

Well, I went home and to bed, and by the morning I'd near forgot all about it. But when I went to the work, there was none to do! All was done already! The horses seen to, the stables cleaned out, everything in its proper place, and I'd nowt to do but sit with my hands in my pockets.

And so it went on day after day, all the work done by Yallery Brown, and better done, too, than I could have done it myself. And if the master gave me more work, I sat down by, and the work did itself, the singeing irons, or the besom, or what not, set to, and with never a hand put to them would get through in no time. For I never saw

Yallery Brown in daylight; only in the darklins I have seen him hopping about, like a will-o-the-wyke without his lanthorn.

To first, it was mighty fine for me. I'd nowt to do, and good pay for it; but by and by, things began to go arsy-varsy. If the work was done for me, it was undone for the other lads. If my buckets were filled, theirs were upset. If my tools were sharpened, theirs were blunted and spoiled. If my horses were clean as daisies, theirs were splashed with muck. And so on. Day in, day out, it was always the same. And the lads saw Yallery Brown flitting about of nights, and they saw the things working without hands of days, and they saw as my work was done for me, and theirs undone for them, and naturally they began to look shy on me, and they wouldn't speak or come near me, and they carried tales to the master, and so things went from bad to worse.

For—do you see?—I could do nothing myself. The brooms wouldn't stay in my hand, the plough ran away from me, the hoe kept out of my grip. I'd thought oft as I'd do my own work after all, so as may be Yallery Brown would leave me and my neighbours alone. But I couldn't. I could only sit by and look on, and have the cold shoulder turned on me, whiles the unnatural thing was meddling with the others, and working for me.

To last, things got so bad that the master gave me the sack, and if he hadn't, I do believe as all the rest of the lads would have sacked him, for they swore as they'd not stay on the same garth with me. Well, naturally I felt bad. It was a main good place, and good pay, too; and I was fair mad with Yallery Brown, as had got me into such a trouble. So before I knew, I shook my fist in the air and called out as loud as I could:

"Yallery Brown, come from the mools; thou scamp, I want thee!"

You'll scarce believe it, but I'd hardly brung out the words as I felt something tweaking my leg behind, while I jumped with the smart of it. And soon as I looked down, there was the tiddy thing, with his shining hair, and wrinkled face, and wicked, glinting black eyes.

I was in a fine rage, and should liked to have kicked him, but it was no good, there wasn't enough of him to get my boot against.

But I said to once: "Look here, master, I'll thank you to leave me alone after this, do you hear? I want none of your help, and I'll have nowt more to do with you—see now."

The horrid thing brak out with a screeching laugh, and pointed his brown finger at me.

"Ho ho, Tom!" says he. "You've thanked me, my lad, and I told you not, I told you not!"

"I don't want your help, I tell you!" I yelled at him. "I only want never to see you again, and to have nowt more to do with you. You can go!"

The thing only laughed and screeched and mocked, as long as I went on swearing, but so soon as my breath gave out, "Tom, my lad," he says, with a grin, "I'll tell you summat, Tom. True's true I'll never help you again, and call as you will, you'll never see me after today; but I never said as I'd leave you alone, Tom, and I never will, my lad! I was nice and safe under the stone, Tom, and could do no harm; but you let me out yourself, and you can't put me back again! I would have been your friend and worked for you if you had been wise; but since you are no more than a born fool, I'll give you no more than a born fool's luck; and when all goes arsy-varsy, and everything a gee—

you'll mind as it's Yallery Brown's doing, though happen you didn't see him. Mark my words, will you?"

And he began to sing, dancing round me, like a bairn with his yaller hair, but looking older nor ever with his grinning wrinkled bit of a face:

"Work as you will,
"You'll never do well;
"Work as you might,
"You'll never gain owt:
"For harm and mischief and Yallery Brown
"You've let out yourself from under the stone."

Ay! He said those very words, and they have ringed in my ears ever since, over and over again, like a bell tolling for the burying. And it was the burying of my luck—for I never had any since. However, the imp stood there mocking and grinning at me, and chuckling like the old devil's own wicked self.

And man!—I can't rightly mind what he said next. It was all cussing and swearing and calling down misfortune on me; but I was so mazed in fright that I could only stand there, shaking all over me, and staring down at the horrid thing; and I reckon if he'd gone on long, I'd have tumbled down in a fit. But by and by, his yaller shining hair—I can't abide yaller hair since that—rose up in the air, and wrapped itself round him, while he looked for all the world like a great dandelion puff; and he floated away on the wind over the wall and out of sight, with a parting skirl of his wicked voice and sneering laugh.

I tell you, I was near dead with fear, and I can't scarcely tell how I ever got home at all, but I did somehow, I suppose.

Well, that's all; it's not much of a tale, but it's true, every word of it, and there's others besides me as have seen Yallery Brown and known his evil tricks—and did it come true, you say? But it did sure! I have worked here and there, and turned my hand to this and that, but it always went a gee, and it is all Yallery Brown's doing. The children died, and my wife didn't; the beasts never fatted, and nothing ever did well with me. I'm going old now, and I shall must end my days in the house, I reckon; but till I'm dead and buried, and happen even afterwards, there'll be no end to Yallery Brown's spite at me. And day in and day out I hear him saying, whiles I sit here trembling:

> "Work as you will,
> "You'll never do well;
> "Work as you might,
> "You'll never gain owt;
> "For harm and mischief and Yallery Brown
> "You've let out yourself from under the stone."

Moowis

HE was the finest hunter, the greatest fighter, the swiftest runner, of all the tribes of the Algonquin. She was the most beautiful, the most skilful, the boldest maiden.

He could summon chieftains' daughters. She was beloved of warriors.

He wooed her. She mocked him.

She told all who listened of how he had come to her, humble, gentle, naked in his heart. The squaws cackled, and the braves jeered, and he lay in his tent and dared not show his tears. The tears chilled his soul.

It was the time for the tribe to move north for the Summer. They broke the Winter camp, and the village was bustle and noise, but still he lay in his tent and would not come out, nor would he speak. So they took the tent from over him, and left him alone on the prairie, while they went north after the deer and the buffalo.

When there was only the level sky to see him, and the silence to hear him, he moved about among the ashes of the dead fires, and the patches of earth, and the forsaken rubbish, gathering a broken bead, a scrap of rotted leather, a twist of rag, a spoilt headdress; and he took them to a sheltered place among the rocks, where some of the Winter's snow still lingered. He gathered the snow, and heaped it, as the village children did, and trimmed it and smoothed it, and rounded a head, and put in stones for

eyes and nose and teeth. Then he stuck the bits of rubbish here and there about the snow, and when he had finished he sang a song.

The tribe watched him come into the camp one cold dawn a week later. He had travelled through the nights to be with them, and by his side was a tall and fierce warrior, a young chieftain of the Cree by the marks on feather and skin. The name of this warrior was Moowis.

She looked on the chieftain, and loved him. Her mother offered the hospitality of their tent, but Moowis said that he was on a journey of hardship and that he must sleep out in the open, with no cover from the frosts of Spring. So she spent her days in pursuit of a chieftain's love, and left him to the stars at night. And she soon came to her desire, for Moowis took her for his bride.

Yet still she could not bring the chieftain to the tent.

"When we reach home, my home," said Moowis, "we shall share everything. Until then, be patient," and he gave her a glittering smile.

The Cree lands were further to the north than the tribe hunted, and Moowis seemed anxious to travel fast, so the new bride and groom took their leave, and her old love, the spurned one, was the last and gayest in the parting.

Moowis urged the way north, and would not allow for her softer strength, and he kept to shadows by day, and made most speed by night. She went with him on bleeding feet, uncomplaining at the hurt, as a chieftain's wife should. She endured the edges of the rocks and the thorns of the woods when they came to the northern mountains. She planned the fine clothes she would wear, and the dressing of her tent, and was happy with Moowis, her lord and her love.

On the last day, the sun rose in a clear sky. The first scents of growing were in the air, and she followed Moowis up a long cliff path, with neither shade nor shelter. The straight back of her husband, which she had never seen bend in all their journey, went before her. His chieftain feathers were proud.

Yet there was something.

His body he pressed to the cliff, and for all his strength, there was less speed to his pace. She could keep with him easily. The doeskin across his shoulders sagged, the sleeves wrinkled, the legs were slack. And in the growing warmth of the sun dark patches spread like sweat.

"Have you the fever?" she said.

But Moowis did not speak again. He stopped, the head-dress fell, and she crouched alone, the chieftain's bride, on the mountain path, over a puddle of melt-water and some rags and feathers drying in the sun.

The Snow Man

One must have a mind of winter
To regard the frost and the boughs
Of the pine-trees crusted with snow;

And have been cold a long time
To behold the junipers shagged with ice,
The spruces rough in the distant glitter

Of the January sun; and not to think
Of any misery in the sound of the wind,
In the sound of a few leaves,

Which is the sound of the land
Full of the same wind
That is blowing in the same bare place

For the listener, who listens in the snow,
And, nothing himself, beholds
Nothing that is not there and the nothing that is.

WALLACE STEVENS

The Lady of the Wood

EINION the son of Gwalchmai was one fine morning walking in the woods of Treveilir when he beheld a graceful slender lady of elegant growth, and delicate feature, and her complexion surpassing every white and red in the morning dawn and the mountain snow, and every beautiful colour in the blossoms of wood, field and hill.

And then he felt in his heart an inconceivable commotion of affection, and he approached her in a courteous manner, and she also approached him in the same manner; and he saluted her, and she returned his salutation; and by these mutual salutations he perceived that his society was not disagreeable to her. He then chanced to cast his eye upon her foot, and he saw that she had hoofs instead of feet, and he became exceedingly dissatisfied.

But the lady gave him to understand that he must pay no attention to this trifling freak of nature. "Thou must," she said, "follow me wheresoever I go, as long as I continue in my beauty."

The son of Gwalchmai thereupon asked permission to go and say good-bye to his wife, at least.

This the lady agreed to. "But," said she, "I shall be with thee, invisible to all but thyself."

So he went, and the goblin went with him; and when he saw Angharad, his wife, he saw her a hag like one grown old, but he retained the recollection of days past, and still

56

felt extreme affection for her, but he was not able to loose himself from the bond in which he was.

"It is necessary for me," said he, "to part for a time, I know not how long, from thee, Angharad, and from thee, my son, Einion." And they wept together and broke a gold ring between them; he kept one half and Angharad the other, and they took their leave of each other, and he went with the Lady of the Wood, and knew not where. A powerful illusion was upon him, and he saw not any place, or person, or object under its true and proper appearance, excepting the half of the ring alone.

And after being a long time, he knew not how long, with the goblin, the Lady of the Wood, he looked one morning as the sun was rising upon the half of the ring, and he bethought him to place it in the most precious place he could, and he resolved to put it under his eyelid; and as he was endeavouring to do so, he could see a man in white apparel, and mounted on a snow-white horse, coming towards him, and that person asked him what he did there; and he told him that he was cherishing an afflicting remembrance of his wife Angharad.

"Dost thou desire to see her?" said the man in white.

"I do," said Einion, "above all things, and all happiness of the world."

"If so," said the man in white, "get upon this horse, behind me." And that Einion did, and looking around he could not see any appearance of the Lady of the Wood, the goblin, excepting the track of hoofs of marvellous and monstrous size, as if journeying towards the north.

"What delusion art thou under?" said the man in white.

Then Einion answered him and told everything how it occurred 'twixt him and the goblin.

"Take this white staff in thy hand," said the man in

white, and Einion took it. And the man in white told him to desire whatever he wished for.

The first thing he desired was to see the Lady of the Wood, for he was not yet completely delivered from the illusion. And then she appeared to him in size a hideous and monstrous witch, a thousand times more repulsive of aspect than the most frightful things seen on earth. And Einion uttered a cry of terror; and the man in white cast his cloak over Einion, and in less than a twinkling Einion alighted as he wished on the hill of Treveilir, by his own house, where he knew scarcely anyone, nor did anyone know him.

But the goblin, meantime, had gone to Einion's wife, in the disguise of a richly apparelled knight, and wooed her, pretending that her husband was dead. And the illusion fell upon her; and seeing that she should become a noble lady, higher than any in that country, she named a day for her marriage with him. And there was a great preparation of every elegant and sumptuous apparel, and of meats and drinks, and of every honourable guest, and every excellence of song and string, and every preparation of banquet and festive entertainment.

Now there was a beautiful harp in Angharad's room, which the goblin knight desired should be played on; and the harpers present, the best of their day, tried to put it in tune, and were not able.

But Einion presented himself at the house, and offered to play it. Angharad, being under an illusion, saw him as an old, decrepit, withered, grey-haired man, stooping with age, and dressed in rags. Einion tuned the harp, and played on it the air which Angharad loved. And she marvelled exceedingly, and asked him who he was. And he answered in song:

"Einion the golden-hearted."

"Where hast thou been?"

"In Kent, in Gwent, in the wood, in Monmouth,
    "In Maenol, Gorwenydd;
"And in the valley of Gwyn, the son of Nudd;
    "See, the bright gold is the token."

And he gave her the ring.

"Look not on the whitened hue of my hair,
    "Where once my aspect was spirited and bold;
"Now grey, without disguise, where once it was
                                    yellow.
"Never was Angharad out of my remembrance,
    "But Einion was by thee forgotten."

But Angharad could not bring him to her recollection.
Then said he to the guests:

"If I have lost her whom I loved, the fair one of
                                    polished mind,
    "The daughter of Ednyfed Fychan,
"Still get you out! I have not lost
    "Either my bed, or my house, or my fire."

And upon that he placed the white staff in Angharad's
hand, and instantly the goblin which she had hitherto seen
as a handsome and honourable nobleman, appeared to her
as a monster, inconceivably hideous; and she fainted from
fear, and Einion supported her until she revived.

And when she opened her eyes, she saw there neither
the goblin, nor any of the guests, nor of the minstrels, nor
anything whatever except Einion, and her son, and the
harp, and the house in its domestic arrangement, and the

dinner on the table, casting its savoury odour around. And they sat down to eat, and exceeding great was their enjoyment. And they saw the illusion which the goblin had cast over them. And thus it ends.

A Voice Speaks from the Well

Gently dip: but not too deepe;
For feare you make the goulden beard to weepe.
Faire maiden white and red,
Combe me smoothe, and stroke my head:
And thou shalt have some cockell bread.
Gently dippe, but not too deepe,
For feare thou make the goulden beard to weep.
Faire maide, white, and redde,
Combe me smoothe, and stroke my head;
And every haire, a sheave shall be,
And every sheave a goulden tree.

GEORGE PEELE

Bash Tchelik

A TSAR had three sons and three daughters, and when he was dying, he told his sons that they should give their sisters in marriage to the first who might come for them.

He died, and shortly after the funeral there was a knocking at the palace gate, and a tearing of the air, and such disturbances of nature that the foundations of the palace quaked. Then came a voice.

"O princes, open the door!"

"Don't open!" cried the eldest brother.

"Don't!" said the second.

"I must open!" said the youngest. And he did so.

Something came in, but what it was the princes could not see, whether it was a fallen star or a coal of hell, and out of the dazzling brightness the voice spoke again.

"I have come for your eldest sister to take her for wife."

"I will not give her," said the first brother.

"I have no time to spare," said the voice. "I must take her now."

"I will not," said the second brother. "How can I give my sister to one I can't see, and whom I do not know, nor can guess?"

But the youngest brother said, "I will give her. Our father's last words were that we should do just this." He took his sister gently by the hand, and led her towards the light. "I hope that she will be a good wife."

Lightning and thunder blinded and deafened the whole palace then, and when it had cleared, both the presence and the sister were gone.

And the next night a voice came again.

"O princes, open the door!"

They were too frightened to resist, and when the light stood on the floor it said, "Give me your second sister."

"I will not!" said the eldest brother.

"I will not," said the second brother.

"I will," said the youngest brother. "It was our father's last wish on earth."

And on the third night, "O princes, open the door!"

"We will not give our sister by night," said the first and second brothers together.

"I will," said the youngest brother. "May you have joy and happiness together."

The next dawn all three princes decided to go out into the world to find their sisters, to be sure that they were happy and well. They travelled for many days until they lost their way in a dark forest, and at nightfall they looked for a place to camp, and they built their fire by the side of a lake. After they had eaten, they settled down to sleep, while the eldest prince kept watch.

At midnight the lake boiled, and the eldest prince saw a black hump driving a wave right for him. It was a water monster, but the prince fought it, and swung his sword through its head. He cut off the ears, and put them in a bag, then he threw the body into the lake and went to sleep.

The whole of the following day the brothers tramped through the forest until they came to another lake at sunset, and there they made a fire, and the second brother stood guard that night. And a monster attacked, as the other had done, but this one had two heads, which the brother split with his sword. He cut off both pairs of ears and put them in a bag, then he slept.

On the third night, by the third lake, the third brother watched, and the third water monster came, and it had three heads. The youngest brother killed the beast, and put three pairs of ears in a bag, and then he slept. Nor had any of the brothers mentioned any of the monsters to each other.

Now they left the forest behind them, and came into a fearsome desert, where the sun burnt them by day, and the winds chilled them by night. They built a fire of dead thorn bush, and while two brothers made a shelter the youngest went off in search of wood for the fire.

He had not gone far when he came to the top of a rocky height, and below him he saw flames in a valley. He climbed down to beg wood of the people there, but when he came near he saw that the fire was burning in the mouth of a cave, and round the fire sat nine giants, roasting two men on spits. A cauldron seethed the limbs of more men, and there were long shapes hanging from hooks in the cave roof.

"Hello!" said the young prince, and he stepped forward into the light. "I have been looking everywhere for you, my friends!"

The giants sized him up, but made no move. "Welcome," they said, "since you are one of us. And since you are one of us, take a joint of this man now, eh? And then you will help us when we go a-foraging, eh?"

"By all means," said the prince, "and thank you."

He joined the circle round the fire, and dipped his hand in the cauldron.

After this supper the giants said that they would have to

go to find their breakfast before they slept, and the prince would come with them.

"Naturally," said the prince. "You will find a dwarf giant very useful, I promise."

"We need not be long," said the biggest giant. "The city is not far away from which we have filled our larder these nineteen years."

When they came to the city, the giants uprooted two pine trees, and put one against the wall. The prince, being small and light, went up the tree, and the giants then gave him the second tree to lean against the wall on the other side.

"I don't quite understand what it is you want me to do," said the prince. "Come and show me."

So one of the giants climbed to the top of the wall, and propped the tree on the city side. The prince drew his sword in the shadow of the parapet, and when the giant bent forward to secure the tree against the wall, the prince took off his head with the sword, and pushed the body from the parapet into the dark of the street below.

"All clear," he said to the giants outside the city, "so up you come: one at a time, please, and don't rush. There's plenty for all."

When the giants were headless, the prince went down into the city. He found the place empty.

But there was one light shining in the city. It came from a window at the top of a tall tower. The prince found the door and the stairway, and climbed to the room. It was furnished with silks and jewels, and on a bed of silver lay a beautiful girl, asleep.

The prince stood, watching, and as he watched, a snake slid through the window and on to the pillow and coiled itself to strike the girl. But the prince drew his dagger and threw it, taking the snake through the head, pinning it to the wall.

"Let no one be able to remove this dagger but me," said the prince. He left the lighted room in the dark city and went back to the cave. There he burnt all that he found, and carried a load of wood to his brothers.

After they had slept and the day had come, they went on, and arrived at the city.

Now it was the habit of the tsar of this city to walk out each morning to view the havoc of the giants, and each morning there were fewer people between the giants' appetites and his only daughter's fair flesh. Yet if she had to be eaten, he would make certain that she was the last, and he had built her a tower, higher than giants could reach, with one stair, narrower than a giant's belly, and there she lived in safety. The giants would have to destroy the tower to reach her, and they would not do that while there were easier meals to be found.

Heavy with grief, the tsar walked about his city, and he entered the street where the pine tree stood against the wall—and there at its foot were tumbled nine headless bodies.

The people crept from their hiding places when they heard the great, joyful shout that the tsar gave, and soon the streets were alive with happiness. Then the snake was discovered, nailed to the wall by a dagger that no one could pull free.

The tsar issued a proclamation that the hero who had killed the giants and saved the life of the tsar's daughter would be honoured above all men, and would have the daughter's hand in marriage.

When the three brothers arrived at the inn by the city gate they found that all the talk was of high deeds, and they were asked if they had ever fallen in with adventures that had called for bravery.

"Well," said the eldest brother, "when we camped by the first lake on our way here through the forest, I stood guard while my brothers slept, and there came a water monster to eat us, but I killed it and cut off its ears." And he opened his bag, and took out the proof of his tale.

"On the second night," said the second brother, "I was attacked by a monster with two heads, and these are the ears to show for it."

"And on the third night," said the youngest, "I won my share," and he tipped six ears out of his bag on to the table. "Yet more than that," said the prince, "I know who sleeps in a silver bed, and I know what is hanging close by on the wall, and I can remove it."

At this, the prince was taken to the presence of the tsar, who made him tell his story in every detail. Then he went to the girl's room in the tower, and lightly pulled the dagger from the wall and put it back in its sheath at his waist.

"You shall be my son," said the tsar, and the prince and the tsar's daughter were married that night.

To the brothers the tsar offered castles, gold and land, but they said that they must continue with their search until they knew where their three sisters were kept and how they fared in the world, and so they rode away.

The prince and his princess were happy for a while, and then he too felt that he could not be at ease until he knew his sisters' fate. He said farewell to his tearful wife, but she called him back. Again he tried to leave, but now her father had heard of what he intended, and the tsar made him prisoner in the palace. He was honoured and loved, but he was not free.

One day, the tsar and all his court were to go hunting, and the prince was left alone with only the servants on duty to look after his needs and his custody. The prince was bored. The fine rooms and corridors were stale to him. He wandered down into the cellars, where he had never been.

The farthest passage of the farthest vaults was blocked with old wine casks. They had been there so long that their hoops had rusted away, their staves shrunk, and the prince soon cleared aside enough for him to see that the passage continued, even though the walls were crumbling with damp and age.

By the light of his lantern he saw a massive door at the end of the passage, and it was not long before he had made a space big enough for him to crawl through over the rotten barrels.

The door was rusted on to its hinges, and was locked, but the prince found a key hanging against the wall under a mat of cobweb, and by using a splintered stave as a lever he managed to turn the lock and then to prise open the door.

The room inside was a dungeon of stifled air, and in the middle of the floor was a fountain of pure water which ran through a golden pipe into a golden basin, and near it a golden cup, rich in jewels and silver work.

But there was more in the dungeon. A man stood against the wall. His legs were bound in iron bands up to his knees, and his arms were bound in iron; and in each corner of the room there were chains fastened about oak beams, and each chain ran to an iron collar about the man's neck, so that he could not move any part of him. His hair and beard hid his face, and lay in the slime about his feet. The prince thought that he must have been dead for centuries, but then he heard a whisper. "Come to me. Do me a deed."

The prince parted the hair over the man's face, and two eyes looked at him in the light.

"Give me water," said the man, "and I shall give you a life."

The prince filled the golden cup and put it to the withered lips.

"What is your name?"

"Bash Tchelik," said the man. "Give me more water, and I shall give you another life."

The prince refilled the golden cup.

"Another drink, for another life," said the man, when the cup was empty.

"Very well," said the prince, thinking that the prisoner was mad with his years of dark.

"Pour this one over my head," said Bash Tchelik, and the prince did so.

Bash Tchelik lifted his arms, and the iron bands snapped like straw. He broke the collar about his neck with one twist. He kicked the iron from his legs. He grew. And as he stepped from the wall, the prince saw that there were great wings folded on his back.

Bash Tchelik went from the dungeon like a black storm, scattering the barrels in the passage, bursting the doors, and when the prince crawled from the cellar he found the palace wrecked and his wife stolen.

When the tsar returned from the hunt he did not blame the prince. "You did not know this man," he said. "I have broken many an army on his lance, and he is not to be killed by any means."

"If he breathes, he can be made to stop breathing," said the prince. "I shall seek him and destroy him."

"Stay here," said the tsar. "I shall look on you as my son, now that I have no daughter, and I shall get you another wife. It is too late in my life for me to spend the years again in binding Bash Tchelik."

"It is not too late in my life," said the prince, and he took horse and left the palace.

He came to a castle, and from a window a girl called to him.

"Stay here, noble prince, and welcome, brother!"

He saw his eldest sister, and they laughed and wept together, and he entered the castle.

"My husband is the king of dragons," she said, "and I am very happy. Our father must have known what was to happen, for the dying see the future, it is said, and you were the oldest in trust if not in years. Now you must go."

"But why?" said the prince. "I have only just this moment found you, and finding was my first quest."

"My husband has sworn that he will kill my brothers if he ever meets them again, because of the discourtesy he met with."

"I shall stay," said the prince.

"Then you must hide," said his sister, and when the king of dragons came home, she asked him: "Dearest husband, would you really kill my brothers if they appeared?"

"The first two," said the king of dragons, "I should roast. But the youngest I should welcome. So let him come out from hiding. I know he is here, for I smell human bones."

The prince told the king of dragons about Bash Tchelik, and the king of dragons said, "Be advised, and stay here with us. On the day that Bash Tchelik escaped from the tsar, I attacked him with five thousand of my dragons, and I managed to escape alive, but only just."

"I must go," said the prince.

"Then take this feather," said the king of dragons, "and if ever you need my help, burn it, and I shall be with you."

The prince set out early the next day, and by evening he had reached the castle where his second sister lived. She was married to the king of eagles, and he too had promised to kill the brothers, except for the youngest, who had treated him graciously.

The prince stayed the night with his second sister and the king of eagles, and when he left, the king of eagles gave him a feather, to burn if he should need help.

And the third evening he came to the castle of the king of falcons, and found his youngest sister there, and the next day he took with him a feather from the king of falcons to strengthen him in his search for Bash Tchelik.

He found his wife in a mountain cave, alone, in rags, tending the fire. "What work is this for a princess?" he said. "Find me Bash Tchelik!"

"Run," said his wife, "before Bash Tchelik finds you. I have no power with him. I am his slave."

"He shall die for that," said the prince, and he put his wife before him on his horse, "but first I shall take you to your father, to be safe while I kill this monster."

He rode away, but there was only weeping from his wife, for she knew Bash Tchelik.

Bash Tchelik caught them before they had gone a mile, and he took the princess from the protection of her husband's sword as a badger takes honey from wild bees.

"Prince," he said, "you have stolen your wife. For that you must die. But I gave you a life, and now you have it." And Bash Tchelik flew home to his cave.

Yet the prince did not let himself be beaten, and he went and took his wife again.

"Prince," said Bash Tchelik, "I gave you another life. You have it."

But the prince went again and took his wife.

"Prince," said Bash Tchelik, "will you be shot with this arrow, or beheaded with this axe?"

"Neither," said the prince. "I choose my other life."

"Remember it is the last," said Bash Tchelik. "The next one is your own."

By now the prince had seen that no earthly weapon would harm Bash Tchelik, so he drew the three feathers from his pocket and burnt them. And at once the hosts of the dragon and the eagle and the falcon were with him, and they fell upon Bash Tchelik.

At the end of the day, the three kings flew unknown with the prince to safety.

"Our people are destroyed, and Bash Tchelik is not hurt," they said. "Give up your wife, since nothing can win her back."

"I can win her," said the prince, but this time he went cunningly, and whispered to his wife:

"All things that live can die. Find out the secret of his life, and I shall lie close and listen."

Bash Tchelik came home in the evening, and the princess said to him, "Tell me where your life is hidden, so that I may guard it the better."

Bash Tchelik laughed, and said, "My life is in my axe."

And when he came home the next day he found the princess kneeling before the axe, which she had draped with silk and adorned with spices.

Bash Tchelik laughed again. "Why do you kneel here?" he said.

"I honour the power that can vanquish falcons and eagles and dragons," said the princess.

"My life is not there," said Bash Tchelik. "It is in my bow."

And the following day, the princess had decked the bow with fine ribbons.

"If I did not know that your husband lay dead upon my battlefield," said Bash Tchelik, "I should trust you the less, but none escaped: so you may know that far from here is a mountain of crystal, and in that mountain there lives a fox; and in that fox there is a raven; and in that raven there is an egg; and in that egg is my life."

"Then I can sleep secure," said the princess.

The prince went straight to the king of dragons, who took him on his back to the distant mountain, and with his fire he split the crystal, and the red fox that had shimmered like a ruby in its clear heart ran out. But the king of eagles

pounced on it from the sky, and ripped the fur a darker red. Up sprang the raven, and fled on the wind, but the king of falcons closed with it, and the talons met in the raven's heart.

The king of falcons brought the raven to the prince.

Across the world, Bash Tchelik woke from his sleep, and sped roaring to the mountain. He found the prince by the broken crystal, fox and raven at his feet, and a smooth, white egg in his hand.

The prince looked at Bash Tchelik. Bash Tchelik looked at the prince. The prince's fingers tightened on the egg. There was a tiny, splintered sound, and the shell was crazed with lines, faint as smoke. The fingers tightened. Yolk ran shining on his wrist.

The Dark Guest

Just once or twice a year he came
At meal-time, and they said:
"Come in," but I could tell their eyes
Begged, "Keep away," instead.

He was a very dirty man—
A child could see as much—
And dirt was bound to be on all
His greasy hands might touch.

The silent men at table moved
To give him lots of room;
But he was brisk and merry as
A cricket in a tomb.

He had a joke for every man
And banter for the maid,
But they all sat as though they were
Grown suddenly afraid.

He ate with hearty appetite,
He drank with right good will,
And then got up and took his way,
Outdoors and down the hill.

And then they scrubbed his cup, as if
It had been lipped by sin,
And said the dark things that their eyes
Had looked when he came in.

But I was not allowed to hear,
"There's time enough for that
When you've grown up," they always said,
And gave my head a pat.

And pushed me from the kitchen door
To run along and play,
And never guessed what thing they made
My playfellow that day.

ERNEST GEORGE MOLL

The Goblin Spider

RAIKO was a great killer of goblins, and the best of his servants was Tsunna.

One day these two were crossing the plain of Rendai when a skull rose in the air before them like a bird from its nest and flew towards a place known as Kagura ga Oka. Raiko and Tsunna followed the skull, and came to a ruined house.

"Warrior-master," said Tsunna, "I'd go careful. I can see a woman in there, through the window, and she's bones old."

Raiko chose a sword from the bundle Tsunna held, the right length for the house, and the right strength for the purpose, and he climbed over the rubble into the building.

The woman stood in the middle of the floor. She was dressed in white, and had white hair. She opened her eyes with a small stick, and the upper eyelid fell back over her head like a hat.

"I am two hundred and ninety winters," she said, "and I serve nine masters, and the house in which you stand is haunted by demons."

"Thank you, mother," said Raiko, and passed into the kitchen. There were holes in the roof, and he could see that a storm was approaching, and as the clouds gathered, so there gathered into the room a pack of goblins, but they were not quite in the world yet, and Raiko did not attack them, for he knew that he would hit only the mist, and they, too, could not hurt him. They soon went.

"Are you safe, master-warrior?" called Tsunna.

"Yes," said Raiko. "An old woman and a few ghosts, that's all."

"Well, look for trouble," said Tsunna. "The old woman has disappeared, but I don't like what's coming now. It's just outside the kitchen."

"Stay where you are," said Raiko, "and keep watch. I'll shout if I need you."

As the storm broke there came into the room the tiny figure of a nun, but her face was two feet in length, and her arms were white as snow and thin as threads. She laughed at Raiko, and disappeared.

Raiko stood his ground in that house all through the storm and that night. The goblins dared not invade the world while he was there, but tried to frighten him with shapes.

Just before cockcrow Tsunna said, "I think we've beaten them."

"This is the dangerous time," said Raiko. "If they don't win before dawn this place will be free of them, and they will have lost a gate into the world."

"I can hear footsteps," said Tsunna, "but I can't see anybody, can you?"

But Raiko could see. A woman entered the room, young, lovely, more graceful than willow branches, and even though he knew that she must be something else, Raiko was held by her beauty. And while he stared, threads enmeshed him. They seemed to come from her hair, or they were her hair, a billowing web of stickiness.

Raiko swept his sword at her, but it moved slowly and the blow was soft. She screamed, and vanished. Tsunna

jumped through the window, and found Raiko with the
sword embedded in the floor planks, and the foundation
stone was broken beneath.

The point of the sword was missing, and along the blade
ran white blood.

In daylight Raiko and Tsunna dismantled the house.
They destroyed things of horror built into the walls, and
under the foundation stone they revealed a hiding place,
and in the dark two eyes glowed like the sun and the
moon. "I am sick," droned a voice. "I am in pain."

Tsunna brought a light, and there below the foundation stone was a monster of many legs, covered with
glistening hair, and with a broken sword point in its belly.

Raiko pulled the creature from the hole and killed it.
When he removed the sword point, nineteen hundred and
ninety skulls poured out, and spiders as big as children.
Raiko and Tsunna had grisly work that day.

To the Tengu Goblins and other Demons

WHEREAS our Commander-in-Chief intends to visit the Nikko Mausolea next April, now therefore you Tengu and other Demons inhabiting these mountains must remove elsewhere until the Commander-in-Chief's visit is concluded.

(Signed) Mizuno, Lord of Dewa.

Dated July 1860

This is a translation of a notice issued by the Japanese Government.

The Secret Commonwealth

" A FEW years gone, Anno 1670, not far from Cirencester, was an apparition: being demanded, whether a good spirit or a bad? returned no answer, but disappeared with a curious perfume and most melodious twang. Mr. W. Lilley believes it was a fairy."

Whether Mr. Lilley was right or wrong, fairies do exist. Our traditions of them seem to be partly a coloured memory of the Stone Age and Bronze Age peoples, who lived in Britain between four thousand and three thousand years ago. Most folk-lore is true in this way. The memory of something that actually happened is passed on by word of mouth, gradually changing, and becoming more exaggerated and fanciful (as gossip still does today), until the memory is forgotten and all that is left is the story. You could say that legends are the gossip of history.

These earlier inhabitants of Britain were small; their houses were round huts, roofed with turf; their weapons were made of flint or bronze, and they were no match for the later Celtic invaders, who had iron swords. It is among the Celts—the modern Cornish, Welsh, Scots, Irish—that fairy beliefs are strongest even now. They were the first to have dealings with the fairies in Britain.

The native people were driven by the invaders into the woods and hills, from which they carried on guerrilla warfare—ambushes and skirmishing raids by night. They were feared for this, and it was believed that they had magical powers. And at this point, they took over the second characteristic that has shaped our ideas of them as fairies today. The solid hill-people started to acquire traditions that had been associated with nature spirits and the souls of the dead.

It is understandable. They came and went like shadows in the night: they lived among the rocks and trees: and their huts, thatched with turf, resembled small hills, or green burial mounds.

It would pay the hill-people to encourage the superstitions. They could not win against iron, face to face, in the open, by day. But night, and fear, made all the difference. A blow-pipe is still more deadly in the jungle than a rifle.

As the centuries went by, the conflict between the races wore itself out. Trade was possible, and marriage, but the hill-people were very slow to give up their own way of life. In fact, they seem to have hung on as a race apart until about a hundred and fifty years ago. The last fairies are supposed to have been a tinker-like group of nomads in Caithness, in the remote north of Scotland, but I think there are still areas where the fairy blood is strong.

They are a stocky people, with broad, flat faces, and heavy brows. They are unruly, bad workers, good poachers and cattlemen, quick-tempered, and usually looked down on as being "common". You will find a lot of them in the hills around Biddulph in Staffordshire, and in the Plynlymon district of Wales. And there is a family in the village where I grew up. My grandfather was once going home across the fields at night, and he found himself caught between two feuding sections of the family, who opened up on each other with shotguns. And I can remember not being allowed to play with one of their boys because he was supposed to be dirty and sly. He probably was. But he could run like a dog, and climb impossible trees, and make wild birds pick breadcrumbs out of his hair.

It is this blend of history and fantasy that makes the traditions so haunting. Fairies were never harmless eaters of jelly and cream buns in toadstool houses. They were called the Good Neighbours, or the People of Peace. And they were called by these names because they were the opposite —for the same reason that we say "Good dog" when we're going to be bitten.

Our present ideas of fairies as winged and dainty are the result of a fashion that spread among writers in the seventeenth century. It suited the writers' purpose to use tiny creatures, and although these minute fairies did exist in legends, they were not the only ones. Fairies came in all sizes from the super-human Children of Danu, who were more like gods, to the Cornish Muryans, as small as ants. (They had once been bigger, but they had done some evil, and were condemned to grow smaller with each generation until they disappeared.) But, generally speaking, the fairies were man-size, or a bit less.

Someone who knew the fairies, and described them as real, and not as folk-lore, was the Reverend Robert Kirk. He was the minister of Aberfoyle, in Scotland, and in 1691 he wrote a textbook on fairies, called *The Secret Commonwealth*. Here is what he says about their weapons.

"Their weapons are mostwhat solid, earthly Bodies, nothing of Iron, but much of Stone, like yellow, soft Flint Spa, shaped like a barbed Arrow-head, but flung like a Dairt, with great Force.

"These Armes (cut by Airt and Tools it seems beyond human) have something of the Nature of Thunderbolt subtilty, and mortally wounding the vital Parts without breaking the Skin; of which Wounds I have observed in Beasts, and felt them with my Hands."

This is an exact description of the prehistoric flint arrowheads that are often preserved as charms in Scotland, and called elf-shot. You will find some in any museum.

Apparently the danger from fairies was so great on certain days of the year that people flocked to church for protection. Mr. Kirk says:

"The Fairies remove to other Lodgings at the Beginning of each Quarter of the Year, and at such revolution of Time, Men have very terrifying Encounters with them, even on High Ways; who therefoir usually shune to travel at these four Seasons of the Year, and thereby have made it a Custom to this Day among the Scottish-Irish to keep Church duely evry first Sunday of the Quarter, to hallow themselves, their Corns and Cattell, from the Shots and Stealth of these wandring Tribes. And many of these superstitious People will not be seen in Church againe till the nixt Quarter begin, as if no Duty were to be learned or done by them, but all the Use of Worship and Sermons were to save them from these Arrows that fly in the Dark."

But there were counter-charms against the fairies besides the power of religion. "For they are terrified by nothing earthly so much as by cold Iron." Yet a charm is no good unless it is used properly, and in the fate of Robert Kirk this is well shown.

An account of what happened is given by his successor in the parish, Doctor Graeme, and also by Sir Walter Scott. Here some of the very best of fairy lore is set down as fact.

"As Mr. Kirk was walking in a fairy hill in his neighbourhood, he sunk down in a swoon, which was taken for death. After the ceremony of a seeming funeral, the form of Mr. Kirk appeared to a relation, and commanded him to go to Grahame of Duchray. 'Say to Grahame, who is my cousin as well as your own,' said Mr. Kirk, 'that I am not dead, but a captive in Fairyland; and only one chance remains for my liberation.

" 'At the baptism of my child, I shall appear in the room, when, if Grahame shall throw over my head the knife which he holds in his hand, I may be restored to the world; but if not, I am lost for ever.'

"True to his word, Mr. Kirk did appear at the christening, and was visibly seen; but Grahame was so astonished that he did not throw his knife over the head of the figure, and so to the world Mr. Kirk has not yet been restored."

But a captive of the Good Neighbours seldom returns, or if he returns, years have passed, although they may have seemed like minutes to him.

This happened to John Jenkinson. He sat down one morning to listen to a bird singing in a tree by a fairy hill. When the bird had finished its song, John got up, and he was very puzzled to find that the tree, which had been a sapling at the beginning of the song, was now a hollow stump. He turned back to his house, but his footsteps grew slower and slower, his shadow bent and trembling, and when he reached his doorstep, John Jenkinson crumbled into a thimbleful of black dust.

It was even worse for Iolo ap Hugh.

In North Wales there is a cave that is said to reach from its entrance on the hillside, "under the Morda, the Ceiriog, and a thousand other streams, under many a league of mountain, marsh and moor" all the way to Chirk castle. And it is also said that whoever goes within five paces of its mouth will be drawn into it by the fairies, and lost. All around, the grass grows thick and rank. Even animals fear the spot. "A fox, with a pack of hounds in full cry at his tail, once turned short round on approaching it, his hair all bristled and fretted like frostwork with terror, and ran into the middle of the pack; as if anything earthly—even an earthly death—was an escape from what was waiting in the cave. And the hounds in pursuit of this fox would not touch him, on account of the smell and gleam that stuck to his coat."

Elias ap Evan, who happened one night to stagger just upon the rim of the cave, was so frightened at what he saw and heard that he arrived home perfectly sober; "the only interval of sobriety, morning, noon, or night, that Elias had been afflicted with for upwards of twenty years. Nor ever after that experience could he get tipsy, drink he never so faithfully to that end."

But one misty Halloween, Iolo ap Hugh, the fiddler, decided to solve the mysteries of the cave. He provided himself with "an immense quantity of bread and cheese, and seven pounds of candles", and ventured in.

He never returned.

Long, long afterwards, at the twilight of another Halloween, an old shepherd was passing close to the place, when he heard a faint burst of melody dancing up and down the rocks above the cave. As he listened:

"The music gradually moulded itself in something like a tune, though it was a tune I had never heard before. And then there appeared at the mouth of the cave a figure well known to me by remembrance. It was dimly visible; but it was Iolo ap Hugh—I could see that at once.

"He was capering madly to the music of his own fiddle, with a lantern dangling at his breast.

"Suddenly the moon cleared through the mist, and I saw poor Iolo for a single moment—oh, but it was clearly!

His face was pale as marble, and his eyes stared deathfully. His head dangled loose and unjointed on his shoulders. His arms seemed to keep his fiddle stick in motion without his will.

"I saw him for that instant at the mouth of the cave, and then, still capering and fiddling, he vanished like a shadow from my sight. But he slipped into the cave in a manner quite different from the step of a living and a willing man. He was dragged inwards like the smoke up the chimney, or the mist at sunrise.

"Poor Iolo. Years passed: all hopes and sorrows for him had not only lost their hurt, but were nearly forgotten. I had gone to live in a village far away across the hills. Then one cold December night, we were all shivering in church as the clerk was beginning to light the candles, when music started suddenly from beneath the aisle. Then it passed faintly along to the end of the church, and died away until I could not tell it from the wind that was careering and wailing all about us. But I knew the tune. I knew it!"

The parson took down the tune from the shepherd's whistling. Here it is.

And to this day, if you go to the cave on Halloween, you may hear this tune as distinctly as you may hear the waves roar in a sea-shell. And it is said that on certain nights in a leap year a star stands opposite the farther end of the cave, and by its rays you can see Iolo, and his—companions.

The Piper of Shacklow

The piper of Shacklow,
The fiddler of Finn;
The old woman of Demonsdale
Calls them all in.

The Adventures of Nera

This Irish story is not only full of the ghostly traditions of fairy lore, but it is also a description of the fairies as real people at war with their neighbours.

ONE Halloween Ailill and Mebd were in Rath Cruachan with their household. They set about cooking food. Two captives had been hanged by them the day before that.

Then Ailill said: "He who would now put a withe round the foot of either of the two captives that are on the gallows, shall have a prize for it from me, as he may choose."

Great was the darkness of that night and its horror, and demons would appear on that night always. Each man of them went out in turn to try that night, and quickly would he come back into the house.

"I will have the prize from you," said Nera, "and I shall go out."

"Truly you shall have this my gold-hilted sword here," said Ailill.

Then Nera went out towards the captives, and put good armour on him. He put a withe round the foot of one of the two captives. Thrice it sprang off again. Then the captive said to him, unless he put a proper peg on it, though he be at it till the morrow, he would not fix his own peg on it. Then Nera put a proper peg on it.

Said the captive from the gallows to Nera: "That is manly, O Nera!"

"Manly indeed!" said Nera.

"By the truth of your valour, take me on your neck, that I may get a drink with you. I was very thirsty when I was hanged."

"Come on my neck, then," said Nera.

So he went on his neck.

"Where shall I carry you?" said Nera.

"To the house that is nearest to us," said the captive.

So they went to that house. Then they saw something. A lake of fire round that house.

"There is no drink for us in this house," said the captive. "There is no fire without sparing in it ever, for the fire is well covered at night. Let us therefore go to the other house, which is nearest us."

They went to it then, and saw a lake of water around it.

"Do not go to that house," said the captive. "There is never a washing-tub, nor a bathing-tub, nor a slop-pail in it at night after sleeping. Let us still go to the other house."

"Now here is my drink," said the captive.

Nera let him down on the floor. He went into the house. There were tubs for washing and bathing in it, and a drink in either of them. Also a slop-pail on the floor of the house. The captive drank a draught from each of them, and scattered the last sip from his lips at the faces of the people that were in the house, so that they all died. Henceforth it is not good to have either a tub for washing or bathing, or a fire without sparing, or a slop-pail in a house after sleeping.

Thereupon Nera carried him back to his torture, and Nera returned to Cruachan. Then he saw something.

The hall of Ailill and Mebd was burnt before him, and he beheld a heap of heads of its people cut off by the warriors who had come raiding from the elfin Mound of Cruachan.

He went after the warriors then into the Mound of Cruachan. The heads were displayed to the king in the Mound.

"What shall be done to the man that came with you?" said one of the chieftains.

"Let him come here to me, that I may speak with him," said the elf king.

Then Nera came to them, and the king said to him: "What brought you with the warriors into the Mound?"

"I came in the company of your host," said Nera.

"Go now to yonder house," said the king. "There is a single woman there, who will make you welcome. Tell her it is from me you are sent to her, and come every day to this house with a burden of firewood."

Then Nera did as he was told. The woman bade him welcome, and said: "Welcome to you, if it is the king that sent you here."

"It is truly," said Nera.

Every day Nera used to go with a burden of firewood to the hall. He saw every day a blind man and a lame man on his neck coming out of the hall before him. They would go until they were at the brink of the well by the hall.

"Is it there?" said the blind man.

"It is indeed," said the lame one.

"Let us go away."

Nera then asked the woman about this. "Why do the blind and the lame man visit the well?"

"They visit the crown, which is in the well," said the woman. "A diadem of gold, which the king wears on his head. It is there it is kept."

"Why do those two go?"

"Not hard to tell," said she. "It is they that are trusted by the king to visit the crown. One of them was blinded, the other lamed."

"Come here a little," said Nera to her, "that you may tell me of my adventures now."

"What has appeared to you?" said she.

"Not hard to tell," said Nera. "When I was going into the Mound, it seemed to me that the Rath of Cruachan was destroyed, and Ailill and Mebd, with their whole household, had fallen with it."

"That is not true indeed," said the woman. "It was all a magic and an enchantment. It was not real, the thing that you saw happen. But it will be real, and it will come true, unless you warn your friends."

"How shall I give warning to my people?" said Nera.

"Rise and go back to them," said she. "They are all still round the same cauldron." (Yet it seemed to him three days and three nights since he had come into the Mound.) "Tell them to be on their guard at Halloween next, for the destruction that you saw will be theirs, unless they turn to destroy the Mound. For I will promise them this: the elf Mound to be destroyed by Ailill and Mebd, and the crown of Briun to be carried off by them."

"How will it be believed of me, that I have gone into the Mound?" said Nera.

"Take fruits of summer with you," said the woman.

Then he took wild garlic with him to his winter, and primrose and golden fern.

"And I shall bear you a son," said the woman. "And you must send a message to me here when your people will come to destroy the Mound, so that you may save us, your family and cattle."

Thereupon Nera went back to his people, and found them round the same cauldron; and he related his adventures to them. And then his sword was given to him, and he was with Ailill and Mebd to the end of another year.

That was the very year in which Fergus mac Roich came from exile from the land of Ulster to Cruachan.

"The time has come, O Nera," said Ailill when Halloween next approached. "Arise and bring your family and cattle from the Mound, that we may go to destroy the Mound."

Then Nera went to his wife in the Mound, and she made him welcome.

"Go now," she said to him, "and take a burden of fire-wood with you to the hall. I have gone there for a whole year in your stead, and I said you were in sickness. And there is also your son yonder."

Then Nera went out, and carried a burden of firewood on his neck.

"Welcome alive from your sickness," said the king of the Mound. "And tend your cattle today."

So Nera went with his cattle that day.

He went back to the house in the evening. "Rise up," said the woman to him, "lest your warriors come. They must come this night at Halloween: for the elf Mounds of Ireland are opened then."

And it was so. Ailill, with the men of Connaught and the black host of exile, went into the Mound, and des-troyed the Mound, and took out what there was in it. And then they took away the crown of Briun. That is the Third Wonderful Gift of Ireland.

Nera was left with his wife in the Mound, and has not come out until now, nor will he come till doom.

A Letter

This is a letter sent to a clergyman, the Reverend Edmund Jones. It is incomplete, but worth printing for its clear details.

March 24th, 1772.

Rev. Sir,

Concerning the apparition I saw, I shall relate it as well as I can in all its particulars.

As far as I can remember, it was in the year 1757, in a summer's day about noon, I, with three others, one of which was a sister of mine, and the other two were sisters. We were playing in a field called Kaekaled, in the parish of Bodvary, in the county of Denbigh, near the stile which is next Lanelwyd house, where we perceived a company of dancers in the middle of the field, about seventy yards from us. We could not tell their numbers because of the swiftness of their motions, which seemed to be after the manner of Morris-dancers (something uncommonly wild in their motions); but after looking some time we came to guess that their number might be about fifteen or sixteen.

They were clothed in red, like soldiers, with red handkerchiefs spotted with yellow about their heads. They seemed to be a little bigger than we, but of a dwarfish appearance.

Upon this we reasoned together what they might be, whence they came, and what they were about. Presently we saw one of them coming away from the company in a

98

running pace. Upon seeing this we began to be afraid and ran to the stile. Barbara Jones went over the stile first, next her sister, next to that my sister, and last of all myself.

While I was creeping up the stile, my sister staying to help me, I looked back and saw him just by me; upon which I cried out, my sister also cried out, and took hold of me under her arm to draw me over; and when my feet were just come over, I still crying and looking back, we saw him reaching after me, leaning on the stile, but did not come over,

Away we ran towards the house, called the people out, and went trembling towards the place, which might be about one hundred and fifty yards of the house; but though we came so soon to see, yet we could see nothing of them.

He who came near us had a grim countenance, a wild and somewhat fierce look. He came towards us in a slow running pace, but with long steps for a little one. His complexion was copper-coloured, which might be significative of his disposition and condition; for they were not good, but therefore bad spirits. The red—of their cruelty; the black—of their sin and misery; and he looked rather old than young.

> The dress, the form, the colour, and the size
> Of these, dear sir, did me surprise;
> The open view we had of them all four,
> Their sudden flight, and seeing them no more,
> Do still confirm the wonder more and more.

Halloween

Hey-How for Halloween!
A the witches tae be seen,
Some black, an some green,
Hey-How for Halloween!

ANON

Great Head and the Ten Brothers

FAR away, and a long time ago, on a high mountain, without trees for shelter, without body or arms for anything, on spindly legs, ran Great Head.

Further away, ten boys lived with their uncle. The elder five brothers were hunters, and the younger five stayed at home.

One evening, the hunters did not come back; and the next day, too, they did not come.

"I shall go to find them," said the biggest of the remaining five, and he set out, but no one saw him again. In turn the others went, until only the youngest and smallest was left, and the uncle would not let him go, for fear of losing all.

The youngest and the uncle hunted together now, and the uncle watched for birds in the tree-tops, and the youngest listened for beasts in the thicket.

"Uncle," said the youngest, "I hear a man in the ground."

"Impossible," said the uncle.

"He's asleep," said the youngest.

"It is a hedgehog snoring," said the uncle. "Dig him up."

But when they scooped the earth from the forest floor an arm was there, and the uncle and the youngest untwined from the roots and the soil a living man, covered in mould, and senseless.

They took him back to their home and washed him, and warmed him, and oiled him with bear's grease, and slowly he awoke, and later he could speak.

"Is it Spring?" he said.

"Not yet," said the uncle. "The snows have melted, but Winter has not gone."

"Then why wake me?" said the mole-man. "I can't go back to sleep now."

"We didn't know," said the uncle.

"You'll have to feed me until my waking time," said the mole-man. "I'm hungry."

So the youngest and the uncle looked after their guest. Once he was properly awake he was much better tempered, but still strange. They took it in turns to sit up at night, rather than have him around unwatched.

The mole-man looked up one evening as a storm roared over the forest. "Do you hear that?" he said. "My brother Great Head is riding the wind. How he shouts! Can you hear him?" The wind screamed. "That's my brother! Oh, it's a long time since we talked together, Great Head and I. Yes, we're overdue for a meeting. I think I'll invite him here to stay for a while."

The uncle was terrified.

"Don't worry," said the mole-man. "Great Head is easy, if you know how to handle him. While I'm gone, fetch in a store of maple-wood blocks. They're his favourite food."

The mole-man set out for Great Head's mountain. He took a bow with him, and on the way he cut some arrows from the root of a hickory-tree. And at midday he arrived at the foot of the mountain, and hid in a bush.

Great Head was perched on a rock, frowning and growling at an owl. "I see thee! I see thee!" he said over and over again. The mole-man crept under the grass to

come as near as possible to his brother. But Great Head of the sharp eyes saw the ruckle of the grass. "I see thee!" The mole-man burrowed as hard as he could. "I see thee! I see thee! Thou shalt die!"

The mole-man drew his bow and shot an arrow at Great Head. The arrow became the size of a tree as it flew, and when it reached Great Head it turned round, without striking him, and sped back to the mole-man. Now it shrank in the air, and dropped into the quiver no bigger than when it had left.

The mole-man ran back to the uncle and the youngest, with Great Head behind him, puffing and snorting on the wing of a hurricane. He dived into the hut, and Great

Head burst in after him. The uncle and the youngest began to batter the head with mallets, but the thin legs shook with laughter, for Great Head recognized his brother and was amused by the trick and the greeting. He ate the maple-blocks, a winter's fire load of them, and was well filled.

Then the uncle begged a favour of his guests, and they said that they knew what it would be, and its answer, and that they would carry it out.

"My nephews," said the uncle.

"My brothers," said the youngest.

"I see them," said Great Head. "I see them."

"They are not far from here," said the mole-man. "A witch has them. Come, youngest, and we shall show their bones."

The youngest and the mole-man climbed into Great Head's hair, and they went springing through the forest to the witch. They found her at her door, and the ground was spread with bones, and she was singing.

When she saw them, the witch spoke the word that turns people into dry bones, but Great Head's hair was too thick for it, and his legs too nimble. They escaped the word, and it turned on the witch and boned her, and what was left the youngest burnt to ashes. Then the mole-man told him to sort out his brothers and to gather them in heaps.

"Great Head and I are going home now," he said. "When we pass by over the trees, I shall call to your brothers and they will hear me."

The youngest stood alone and listened to the nearing storm, and out of it a voice cried to the bones, and they rose and were men. "I see them! I see them!" howled the wind.

And soon after, it was Spring.

The Trade that No One Knows

THERE was once an old man, and he had an old wife, and they had one son. They worked hard all their lives to bring up the child fit and strong, and denied him nothing that they wanted him to have. He was their future, for they reckoned that, after all they had done for him, he would spend his years of strength in looking after them in their age.

But when he became a man, the son said to his parents, in the way he was accustomed to speak to them, since it was how they had brought him up:

"I want to get married. Go to the king and tell him I want his daughter."

"Paul, are you mad?" said his mother. "How can we go from our poor hut and our lean table to the banquets of the king and fetch you his daughter?"

"If you don't," said Paul. "I shall leave home."

So the mother was frightened, and she made a wedding cake to placate her son, and left him gazing at it while she went to see the king.

She had put on her best clothes, but when she stood in the palace yard she saw that her clothes were nothing more than clean rags, and she felt ashamed.

She was too ashamed to go forward, and too ashamed to go back, and she might have stayed there for ever if the king had not spoken to her.

"What is it you want from me, old woman?" he said.

And with her shame, and her nervousness and her fear of her son, she said, in a whisper, "Nothing."

"Have you come for charity?" said the king.

"Oh yes! Oh yes!" said the old woman.

So the king told his treasurer to give her ten gold crowns and the old woman went home. "Paul will never leave us when he sees the gold crowns," she said to herself. "He'll stay with his mother."

But Paul kicked the money out of her hand, and shouted, "It's his daughter, not his money I want! Go and get her for me!"

His parents cowered by the door.

"Or else I shall leave home today."

They begged him not to desert them in their old age, but he would not listen, so the old woman had to promise to go again to the king the next morning.

"What is it now?" said the king.

And the old woman was as timid as she had been before, and remembered the previous day as well.

"Nothing," she said. "Nothing, please."

"'Nothing' was ten crowns yesterday," said the king, and he gave her ten crowns more.

"Where is the princess?" said Paul.

"Never mind the princess," said his mother. "Look at the money. Now we can find you a nice girl for a wife."

"You don't want me to marry the king's daughter," said Paul. "You've been tricking me all the time."

"What kind of a house is this to bring a princess to?" said his mother.

"I shouldn't bring her to this house," said Paul. "I should build one for myself."

"And leave us to die?" cried his parents. "Such gratitude!"

"But now," said Paul, "since you have tricked and

cheated me, I shall leave here in the morning. No! I shall leave now." And he made to open the door, but his parents clung to him, and reminded him of all the years they had spent in rearing him, and of their loneliness, and of how everything was done for his happiness.

"Then fetch me the princess," said Paul, "tomorrow without fail."

So there was nothing for the old woman to do but to go to the king in the morning.

And the king said, "What do you want now?"

"Please," said the old woman.

"Not more money," said the king. "There must be something else that brings you to the palace every day with fear on you. Answer me the truth now, or your life may not last."

So the old woman was made to tell the king that her son wanted to marry the princess.

"Then," said the king, "they shall marry: if my daughter is also willing."

And the princess said, "I don't mind—provided that the young man first learns the trade that no one knows."

This pleased the mother greatly, and the king gave her another ten gold crowns and sent her home.

"Where is the princess?" said Paul, and he took up his pack, which he had filled with wedding cake to feed him on his travels. "I told you I would not stay unless you brought her with you."

"I have not brought her," said his mother, "and you will stay. The princess agrees to marry you—but only when you have learnt the trade that no one knows. And since no one knows, then you can put down that pack and give over with your grand ideas. Bring in some logs. My knees are cold."

"Bring them yourself, mother," said Paul. "Father will help you. I am going to find where I may learn the trade that no one knows. Thank you for all you have done for me, and for my wedding cake."

And he closed the door on their wailing anger, and journeyed into the forest.

He journeyed for many weeks and months, but found no teacher of the trade he would learn, and he sat down one evening in a thicket to rest his tired legs and to eat the last of the cake.

A hag came up to him, and said, "You are wretched and weary: why so?"

"You can't help me, and I'm too spent to tell you," said Paul.

"Perhaps I can tell you, then," said the hag. "If you go straight on through the forest you will find what you are looking for."

Paul jumped up, no tiredness now, and ran straight on through the forest. Soon he came to a castle, and four giants rushed out to meet him, shouting, "Do you want to learn the trade that no one knows?"

"Of course," said Paul. "That is why I have come here."

The giants took him into their castle, and at dawn the next day they said that they were going out hunting, and that while they were away Paul must not go into the room on the first floor of the castle.

But the moment he was alone Paul thought: I've made a big mistake in letting them bring me inside this place, and I probably shall never see the world again, so I may as well see this room they think is so important.

He climbed the spiral staircase until he found the first door in the wall, and he opened it. Inside the room was a golden ass by a golden manger.

"Come and take the halter from my head," said the ass, "and hide it under your shirt. If you ever understand its use, then it will be of use to you."

Paul took the halter, and when the giants came back from their hunting they asked him if he had entered the room.

"No," said Paul.

"Yes!" said the giants. "We know!" And they thrashed him with ash sticks, and if he had not been wearing the halter over his ribs he would have been crushed by the blows.

The next morning the giants again went out hunting, but before they left they warned Paul not to go into the room on the second floor of the castle.

I feel half dead already, after last night, thought Paul. Another half won't make that much difference. And he climbed the stair to the second door.

Inside the room sat a beautiful girl. She wore gold and silver, and she was mounting diamonds in every lock of her hair. She sat with her face a little from Paul, and she seemed not to have noticed him, so after looking at her for a long time he turned to leave.

"Take this key," she said, "and guard it. And if you ever understand its use, it will be of use to you." And she gave him a golden key from her waist.

The giants came home. "Did you go to that room?" they said.

"No."

"Yes! We know!" And they clubbed him down, and beat him worse than before.

"If you go into the room on the third floor," the giants said as they left the castle the next morning, "we shall not have mercy on you at all. You will be dead."

I'm not likely to survive, as it is, thought Paul: so let's see what's in that room. I bet it's treasure.

It was heads. The room was piled with human heads. Some had been there a long time, others not very long. They were all the heads of young men—and there was a space waiting for one more.

Paul went back to the stair, but one of the heads called out to him.

"Don't go! You are the first visitor we have ever had! Talk to us!"

"Talk to us!" they all mumbled.

"What shall I say?"

"Tell us why you are here," they chattered.

"I came to learn the trade that no one knows," said Paul.

"So did we! So did we!"

"Then what is the trade?"

"We do not know! We do not know!"

"You can never know if you obey the giants," said the first head. "We were so keen to learn that we never went to the rooms while the giants were out, and on the third night the giants said we should never learn, and cut off our heads."

Paul asked what he ought to do.

"Take this chain," said the head. And it grunted and rocked across the floor towards him, dragging a chain between its teeth.

"It is only an iron chain," said Paul, bending down to look at it. "Haven't you a gold one?"

"If you ever understand its use, it will be of use to you."

"Take it! Take it!" shouted the other heads, and they began to rattle and jump.

Paul took the chain quickly, and locked the door behind him.

This time the giants did not even bother to ask. They set about Paul as soon as they came in, and then they threw him out of the castle.

"Find your princess now," they said. "You have learnt the trade that no one knows."

Paul limped back home through the forest. Well, he thought, if that's the case, then these bruises will have been worth it: but I wish I knew what I've learnt!

When he stood outside the palace he felt very unsure of himself. He was dirty and ragged, and he had no idea what to say to the princess. "At least I don't have to go in stinking," he said. And he stripped off his shirt to wash himself in the brook that ran below the palace wall. Under the shirt was the golden halter, and he unwound it and dropped it on the earth.

Immediately a caparisoned horse stood before him. He unwound the chain, and dropped that.

A hare and a greyhound appeared. And Paul was dressed in hunting green, astride the caparisoned horse, and the greyhound chased the hare.

And as they all passed below the high towers the king looked out and saw the splendour of the huntsman, and he sent heralds out to invite him to banquet at the palace.

Paul heard the riders behind him, and thought that he was being pursued, so he shook the halter and the chain, and the horse, the greyhound and the hare vanished, and he found himself sitting on the ground, dressed in his old clothes. The riders passed him by, and later returned to the king to say that the huntsman had outrun them on his horse of the wind.

Paul now went back to his parents' hut, and after a good sleep he said to his father, "I am going to practise what I have learnt. When I have become a fine chestnut mare, take me to the palace. The king will buy me, but whatever you do, don't sell the halter, or else I shall be a horse for ever."

Paul shook the halter, and his father led off to market the finest chestnut mare that the city had ever seen. He asked such a high price for the mare that no one could afford to buy, and the news of it reached the king. He went to the market place, and as soon as he saw the mare he knew that he must have it for his stables. He gave the father the price that was asked, and ten gold crowns on top.

"I am afraid that Your Majesty can't have the halter," said the father.

"No matter," said the king. "I shall have one made of gold and diamonds."

When the father arrived home he shook the halter, and soon after nightfall his son came through the doorway. Next morning the city was full of the news that the king's new chestnut mare, for which he had paid the highest price in memory, had gone from her stall.

When the wonder had died down, Paul took his father to the palace, and close beneath the wall he looked for a firm piece of level ground, and stood on it.

"Take this key, father," he said, "and shake it. Sell me to the king—but whatever you do, don't sell the key."

The father shook the key, and below the palace wall, on a piece of firm and level ground, stood the finest church in the land.

When the king saw this church he sent out his heralds to find who had built it so quickly, and they came back and said that it was the work of a holy man, clothed in rags, who was willing to sell the church to the king for thirteen chests of treasure.

The king sent his heralds back to bargain with the holy man, and while they were doing so, the hag that had directed Paul to the giants came up, and she saw at once what was happening. Now this hag had herself learnt the trade that no one knows, and she was astonished to find that Paul had survived the giants and that she had a rival in the knowledge. So she joined in the bidding, against the king's men. She waited until the king had offered seventeen chests of treasure, then she offered ten times that. The father was so confused that he forgot to keep hold of the key, and the hag was far away in the crowd before he remembered.

He ran after her, but she would not give up the key. "It is mine," she said. "It belongs to the church, which I have paid so much for."

The father seized the old woman by the neck and began to throttle her. In the swaying and fighting she dropped the key, and it changed into a dove, and soared over the palace wall into the gardens.

The hag became a hawk, and stooped upon the dove, but the dove became a garland and fell into the hands of the princess, who was walking in the rose arbours. The hag resumed her shape, and begged the princess for the garland. "For luck," she said.

But the princess would not.

The hag tried to snatch the flowers, but they turned into millet seed, and scattered across the flagstones. The hag became hen and chickens, and pecked at the seed, but the seed was a fox, and it ate the hen and its chicks.

Then the fox became Paul.

"I come for your hand," he said. "I have travelled the world to learn the trade that no one knows."

"It seems that you have learnt it," said the princess.

And there are still descendants of these two living today, and they worship at an old church, which is never locked, because the key to it was a young man who married a princess after he had learnt, for love of her, the trade that no one knows.

A Charm against Witches

Black-luggie, hammer-head,
Rowan-tree, and red thread
Put the warlocks to their speed.

Tarn Wethelan

ARTHUR kept Christmas at Carlisle, and with him Guenever, the queen, and the knights of the Table, Sir Launcelot and Sir Kay were there, and Sir Banier and Sir Bore, Sir Gareth and Sir Tristram the Gentle, and Arthur's nephew, Sir Gawaine White Hawk.

Yet the court was listless, for such was the might of Arthur that no evil was done in the land. Armour rusted, muscles slackened, the patience of the king grew thin. Arthur took no quests upon himself. His fame lay in the power of his knights. His work was as a peace-bringer, but in peace he found no ease.

He spilled the wine across the board. "The year is almost gone," he shouted, "and no perils! What will the world have of us if we sit at home like women? My mind rots in idleness!"

"Patience," said the doorward. "Here comes your adventure."

A fair woman stood in the hall. Her gown was torn and stained with grass and blood, her hair unpinned and tangled with leaves.

"A boon," she said. "A boon, King Arthur, I seek of you."

"Whatever it may be, you shall have it," said the king.

"A boon, in your Christmas of mirth and honour," said the woman. "Kill me a man."

"What man?" said the king. "And for what ill?"

"A carl knight," she said, "who has shorn my love and me."

"How was it?" said Arthur.

"My love was a courteous knight," she said, "and we were betrothed. Yet as we rode near Tarn Wethelan my love was taken by a dark baron, a giant he seemed in the valley, twice the size of a normal man, in black armour, and he fought with a mace. He bade my love leave me, and when he would not, but tried to save me, the carl struck him down. I think there is some spell of magic there, for my love could not lay a blow upon the man, and though I cried for mercy I was ill-used. And when he set me free, this giant said: "Go to Arthur in Carlisle, and beg for vengeance. And tell that love-spent king to meet me if he dare.""

Up leapt Arthur then, and no one spoke in the hush of that insult. "I swear by dale and hill," said Arthur, "that I shall not quit this rough baron until I see his blood. Let no one go with me, nor in my stead. He has injured this fair lady, but he has done worse to me."

Arthur mounted his horse and rode to Tarn Wethelan, beneath snow crests and ice-clad rocks, through the winter world of Cumberland until he reached the lake. Beside it was a castle, many towered and bright with flying pennants.

Arthur drew his sword. The note of his horn rang in the frozen air. The drawbridge opened; the portcullis slid upwards; and the knight came, black in armour and trappings and horse and mace.

His mace lay on his shoulder, and his other hand was on his hip. He spoke no word, but came on for Arthur, slowly, unguarded, disdainful.

"Dress your shield!" cried Arthur. But the shield bounced behind the man's neck.

"Defend yourself, or yield!"

But the black figure did neither.

"Then die a coward!" said Arthur, and lifted his sword. His sword stuck in the air as if in a log. He could not move it.

The giant rode up.

"What shall I do with you, Arthur the king?" he said. "There are many knights and princes at work for me. Would you be a scullion? Or a stable lad? Would you scour a privy? What would you be?"

The king hung from his sword. His hand was fast to it.

"I am Arthur," he said, "no soldier taken in fight to be your slave."

"Then yield without fight," said the giant, "and accept my terms."

"That is no less a shame to me," said Arthur.

"You do not know my terms," said the giant. "If I take you now, you shall be my serving man. But if you accept my terms, you shall have one chance to win."

"Then that is my choice," said Arthur, "and it is no choice, but the game of a wretched knight with a captive."

"It may be," said the giant. "My terms are that if I let you free now, you shall return here on New Year's Day, with the answer to my question, or I take your land and throne."

"And the question?" said Arthur.

"Bring me word what thing it is that women most desire."

So Arthur gave his promise to return on New Year's

Day, and he rode from Tarn Wethelan like a dead man. And he would have been dead before he reached Carlisle, either from shame at the tale he would have to tell, or from his own sword, rather than live the life of a slave, but he remembered that he had given his promise to the knight, and he could not break it even for death. Yet still he could not face his court. He turned from the path, and set off into the wilderness to ask what women most desired.

Some people told him riches, pomp, or state; mirth; or flattery; clothing bright and fine; some a vigorous knight. And all this Arthur wrote down on parchment and sealed with his ring. But no answer was enough in itself. He found as many as he cared to write and all were different.

On New Year's Eve, heavy with doubt, he retraced his journey to Tarn Wethelan. And as he rode over a high moor he saw a woman sitting between an oak and a green holly, and she was clad in red scarlet.

Her nose was crooked, and her chin stood all awry. She had hair lank as snakes, a hump on her back, one eye turned to the clouds, the other low on her cheek. She was the worst formed woman that Arthur had ever seen, and he tried to ride past without having to look at her.

"Good day, King Arthur," she said.

But the king appeared to be deaf.

"What knight are you," she said, "that you will not speak to me? I was seemly in my greeting, though not in my aspect, and you should speak to me, King Arthur, for I may chance to ease your pain, although I am foul to see."

"If you will ease my pain," said Arthur, "and help me in my need, then you can ask of me whatever you will, and it shall be yours, O grim lady."

"Do you swear that upon the Rood?" said the old woman.

"Upon the Rood, and the Blessed Nails," said Arthur.

"Why, then I shall tell you," she said. "What women most desire is—their own way. And now, what I desire, King Arthur, is a young and handsome knight for bridegroom. Bring one from your court."

"I have given my word," said Arthur. "You shall have your knight. Believe me."

"I do," she said. "Now go on your way. It will soon be the New Year, King Arthur."

He came to Tarn Wethelan in the first daylight of the year. The giant stood waiting, stiff and strong, his mace gleaming with frost.

Arthur gave him the sealed parchments, and the giant tore them open. He read each one and his breath came white from his nostrils.

"Wrong!" he said. The parchments tumbled across the snow like dead leaves. "All wrong! Now yield you, Arthur, and your lands, forfeit to me. This is not your pay, sir king, nor your ransom! Mine!"

"Wait," said Arthur.

"No!" said the knight, and cried himself a king.

"Wait," said Arthur. "Last evening, as I came over a moor, I saw a lady sitting between an oak and a green holly, and she was clad in red scarlet. She said all women will have their will; that is their chief desire."

"An early vengeance on her!" roared the giant. "She who walks on yonder moor! It was my sister told you this!"

"If she is your sister, it is no matter to me, unless her answer was wrong," said Arthur.

"It was not wrong," said the giant knight. "Go your way, Arthur. I shall remember that I was once nearly King of Britain. You are free."

Though free, Arthur rode sadly. And the closer he came
to Carlisle, the sadder he became.

"What news? What news?" Guenever called from the
battlements. "Oh, my lord Arthur, what adventure have
you had?" And all the knights came out to hold his horse
and to help him from his armour. "What news? What
news?"

"Where did you hang the carl?" said Launcelot. "Or
where have you displayed his head?"

But Arthur did not answer, and they thought that he was
weary from the riding and sore from the battle, so they
took him inside and bathed him and put new robes on
him, and prepared a feast.

"The carl is safe for me," said Arthur at last. "He is free
from mortal attack. His castle stands on magic ground, and
is fenced with many a charm. I was made to bow to him,
and to yield me to him; and but for a loathly lady I should
have lost my land."

Then Arthur told of his adventure, and the knights of
that Table were as shamed as he. "There is more," said
Arthur, "and it is the sorrow of my life. In return for her
answer I promised that she should marry a young and
courtly knight. And one of you must do this, or mark me
a word-breaker to the world."

The knights stood back from Arthur, but Sir Gawaine
spoke. "I shall be your ransom," he said. "Be merry."

"No, Gawaine!" said King Arthur. "You are my own
sister's son. You are the last I would have married to the
creature. You have not seen her, Gawaine, you have not
seen."

"I'll take her, uncle, for your sake."

"Thanks, thanks, good Gawaine," said Arthur, in his
heart relieved, and in his manner unable to conceal it, so

that the queen Guenever turned her face aside. "A blessing on you, Gawaine," said Arthur, "and tomorrow we'll have knights and squires, and we'll have hawks and hounds, none sparing, and we'll away to the green forest in pretence of the hunt, and go and fetch your bride."

Sir Kay laughed as if he were drunk.

And the next morning they went to the forest; Sir Launcelot and Sir Steven, Sir Banier and Sir Bore, Sir Tristram the Gentle, and at the head was Sir Kay. And as they rode over a moor they came upon the lady, sitting between an oak and a green holly, and she was clad in red scarlet.

When Sir Kay saw her face he nearly fell from his horse.

"Ai! Gawaine!" he said. "What a snout! Whoever kisses that must stand in fear of his kiss!"

"Yet one of our court must marry her to wife," said Gawaine. "Will it be you?"

"Marry the ill-favoured witch?" said Kay. "No, no, Gawaine White Hawk: first come, first served! She is bespoke, and I would not stand between you for the world or heaven or hell!"

And all the knights took up their hawks in haste, and became busy with their hounds, and some pretended to catch a scent and rode off with great huloo and blowing of horns.

"For a little foul sight and misliking," said Arthur, "you should not turn her away."

Then Sir Gawaine brought up the lady before him on his horse's neck, and so they went back to Carlisle.

That night was the wedding of Sir Gawaine. He placed the gold ring on the gnarled, grey hand, and at the feast he led her to the first dance, and such was his courtesy that no one sneered at the sight of the hobbling bride and the young groom, and he pledged her in the cup, and gently cleaned her chin when it ran with the wine that her slack mouth could not hold.

Torches lit them to their wedding chamber, and by the light of the dying fire Sir Gawaine stood a long time at the window, seeing the clean, white hills under snow, and the young moon, and the peaceful, ageless stars. No echo of revels came from the hall. The castle was silent.

His bride stirred the fire, and the room spurted with yellow light. He moved his head stiffly to look at her.

She was watching him. He knew her by the silver gown, and the blue silk at her waist, and the jewels in her hair— but by nothing else. For he looked at the most beautiful woman in the world; young and tall and lithe; and she was crying with happiness.

"Oh, Gawaine!" she said. "Oh, my love!"

"What? What, lady?" was all he could say.

"I am under a spell," she said, "to be myself for half the day, and to be the old woman for the other hours."

"Why did you not say?" cried Gawaine.

"I must be accepted for my worst," she said. "The man that will marry me then is the man I can trust; no other. And you are the man. And for that you shall have the choice—to have me fair by day or by night, as you will. Choose, now."

"You are more dear to me than moon or stars," said Gawaine. "With your light the darkness will be as day, so let us have our love together privately. Be fair at night for me."

"Oh, Gawaine," she said, "are you this selfish? I am the same beneath, by night and day, the same love, the same care. Am I to be hideous when all are present? Is Kay to jeer and stop his nose at me? When the ladies of the court sew their fine clothes, are my fingers to be claws? May I not take my place and be admired?"

"Hush," said Gawaine, and drew her close to him. "I am so bemused that I cannot think. Let the choice be yours, my love, and have your will."

"My will!" she said. "That is the answer to break the spell. When one man shall give me my will, then I am free from enchantment and for ever fair! The spell is broken that was laid on my brother and me, to make me hideous and him cruel. From this moment I shall be your gentle wife, and he shall be a valiant knight."

In such a way did the black giant of Tarn Wethelan find release, and the grim lady of the moor win the White Hawk: and of her he was as glad as grass would be of rain.

All in Green went My Love Riding

All in green went my love riding
on a great horse of gold
into the silver dawn.

four lean hounds crouched low and smiling
the merry deer ran before.

Fleeter be they than dappled dreams
the swift sweet deer
the red rare deer.

Four red roebuck at a white water
the cruel bugle sang before.

Horn at hip went my love riding
riding the echo down
into the silver dawn.

four lean hounds crouched low and smiling
the level meadows ran before.

Softer be they than slippered sleep
the lean lithe deer
the fleet flown deer.

Four fleet does at a gold valley
the famished arrow sang before.

Bow at belt went my love riding
riding the mountain down
into the silver dawn.

four lean hounds crouched low and smiling
the sheer peaks ran before.

Paler be they than daunting death
the sleek slim deer
the tall tense deer.

Four tall stags at a green mountain
the lucky hunter sang before.

All in green went my love riding
on a great horse of gold
into the silver dawn.

four lean hounds crouched low and smiling
my heart fell dead before.

e. e. cummings

Hoichi the Earless

THERE once lived at the Amidaji temple a blind priest called Hoichi. He was famous for his speaking of poetry and for his playing of the lute, and his greatest love was to recite the stories of far-off battles.

One night Hoichi was sitting alone on the verandah of the temple. It was a warm evening, and very still, and Hoichi sang to himself the story of the great war between the Taira and Minamoto clans, which had been fought close by the temple seven hundred years before.

Behind the notes of his lute Hoichi listened to the sound of footsteps. Someone crossed the back garden of the temple. Then a deep voice spoke below the verandah. "Hoichi," it said. "Hoichi."

"I am here," said Hoichi. "What do you want?"

"My lord is staying close by," said the stranger, "with many noble followers, and he has come to visit the site of the Battle of Dan-no-ura, where the Minamoto slew the Taira. He has heard how well you sing that tale, and he has commanded me to escort you to him. Bring your lute, and follow me."

"Sir, I am blind," said Hoichi.

"Then I shall guide you," said the voice, and Hoichi's wrist was taken in a hard grip. "My lord and his assembly await your presence."

Hoichi shuffled on his sandals and took up his lute, and

went with the noble samurai. He heard the clank of armour as they walked.

They went some little way, and then the samurai called for a gate to be opened. Hoichi heard the unbarring of iron. Once through the gate, there came the sound of many hurrying feet, and Hoichi was led up some steps, and at the top his guide ordered him to remove his sandals. A woman then took his hand, and he felt himself to be in a vast apartment, where a great company was assembled. He heard voices murmuring, and the stiff movement of silk. The woman brought him to a seat, and the room fell silent. Hoichi began the story of the Battle of Dan-no-ura.

His skill made the strings of his lute give the sound of oars, the clash of ships, the shouting of men, the noise of surging waves and the whirring of arrows. He felt the room take up the thrill of war, and when he came to the end, to the final massacre of the women and children of the Taira, the company wept.

"My lord is well pleased," said the woman, "and commands you to play before him for six nights. The samurai will come for you at the temple at the same hour tomorrow." She took him to the steps, and Hoichi went in the same hard grip back to the verandah and the warm night.

"Tell no one of your visit," said the samurai, and left him.

The next evening Hoichi went again to play his lute for the fine assembly, but his fellow priests noticed his absence from prayer, and when he was missing from his duties a second time they questioned him, but Hoichi said that he had important private business to attend to.

The priests were not satisfied, and they kept a secret watch on Hoichi. When he left the temple they followed him through the night, but he walked too quickly for them in the darkness, and they lost him. They searched everywhere for Hoichi about the district, but no one had seen him, and they were making their way back to the temple when they heard the sound of Hoichi's lute.

They put out their lanterns and crept towards the sound. It came from the cemetery of the temple, where the Taira clan had been buried after Dan-no-ura. And there they found Hoichi. He sat by the tomb of the Taira Emperor, Antoku Tenno, and all around him were flames, like candles.

"Hoichi!" cried the priests. But Hoichi did not hear them. They called again, and then they braved the lights and went to him and shook him by the arm.

"How dare you!" said Hoichi. "When I am playing for a noble lord!"

"Hoichi, you are playing for the dead!" said the priests.

"Nonsense!" said Hoichi. "I am here in this palace, singing the Battle of Dan-no-ura, as I have done these nights past."

The priests argued no more, but took Hoichi by force back to the temple.

Now Hoichi knew his danger. For by his skill he had conjured the ghosts, and each night he gave them more life from his art. They took substance from his lute magic, and were growing in power.

Before sunset the next day, the priests began their rites. They stripped Hoichi, and wrote holy texts and prayers over all his body. Then they laid him on the verandah.

"Be silent, very still," they said, "and meditate. If you do these things, you will be free of the dead."

And they left him, and went to pray for his safety.

Hoichi did not move.

Towards midnight the footsteps came across the garden, and the voice spoke. "Hoichi." No answer. "Hoichi, my lord awaits your music. Hoichi!"

Hoichi lay still.

"Where is the priest?" said the voice, and Hoichi felt the verandah bend under the weight of the samurai, and the footsteps walked up and down—and stopped beside him. Hoichi was terrified, but he made no sound.

"Ah," said the samurai, "here is the lute, but where is the player? I see no man, only two ears. Well, they are better than nothing. I'll take them to my lord."

The footsteps died away, and Hoichi kept his silence, though the pain could hardly be borne, and the priests found him in the morning, free from ghosts.

"It is difficult to write on ears," said the priests.

Meeting in the Road

In a narrow road where there was not room to pass
My carriage met the carriage of a young man.
And while his axle was touching my axle
In the narrow road I asked him where he lived.
"The place where I live is easy enough to find,
Easy to find and difficult to forget.
The gates of my house are built of yellow gold,
The hall of my house is paved with white jade,
On the hall table flagons of wine are set,
I have summoned to serve me dancers of Han-tan.
In the midst of the courtyard grows a cassia-tree,
And candles on its branches flaring away in the night."

Chinese: First Century B.C.
Translated by ARTHUR WALEY

Ramayana

Adapted from the Translation of ANANDA K. COOMARASWAMY

RAMAYANA is special. It is the great Hindu epic, probably three thousand years old, and about forty times the length of the version given here. I have tried to extract the main thread of many that run through the story.

A few words may need explanation:

Gandharvas are musical spirits.

Garuda is a divine bird.

Rudra is one of the names of Shiva, who, with Vishnu, is among the greatest of the gods.

Rakshasas, yakshas and asuras are all demons, continually at war with both gods and men.

I. RAMA AND SITA

I

THERE was once a great and beautiful city called Ayodhya—that is, "Unconquerable"—in the country of Koshala. There all men were righteous and happy, well read and contented, truthful, provided with goods, self-restrained and charitable and full of faith.

Its king was Dasharatha, a man amongst men as the moon amongst the stars. His ministers were such as could keep their counsel and judge of things finely; they were well versed in the arts of policy and ever fair-spoken.

Only one of Dasharatha's dreams was unfulfilled: he had no son to carry on his line. Because of this, after many vain austerities, he determined at last on the greatest of all offerings—a horse sacrifice; and calling the family priests, he gave all necessary orders for its undertaking. Then he went to the inner rooms of the palace and told his three wives what had been set afoot, whereat their faces shone with joy, like lotus flowers in early spring.

When a year had passed, the horse that had been turned free came back, and the sacrifice was completed, and there was great festivity and gladness. The priest told the king that four sons would be born to him, perpetuators of his race; at which sweet words the king rejoiced exceedingly.

II

Now at this time all the gods were there assembled to receive their share of the offerings made, and being assembled together they approached Brahma, the Creator of the World, with a petition.

"A certain wicked rakshasa named Ravana greatly oppresses us," they said, "whom we suffer patiently because you have granted him a boon—not to be slain by gandharvas, or yakshas, or rakshasas, or gods. But now his tyranny becomes past endurance, and, O Lord, you should devise some method to destroy him."

To them Brahma replied: "That evil rakshasa disdained to ask from me immunity from the attack of men: by man only he may and shall be slain."

Thereat the gods rejoiced. At that moment there arrived the great God Vishnu, clad in yellow robes, bearing mace and discus and conch. Him the gods reverenced, and prayed him to take birth as the four sons of King Dasharatha for the destruction of the wily and irrepressible Ravana.

Then Vishnu, that one of the lotus eyes, making of himself four beings, chose Dasharatha for his father, and disappeared. In a strange form, like a flaming tiger, he reappeared in Dasharatha's sacrificial fire and, greeting him, named himself as the messenger of God.

"Do you, O tiger amongst men," said Vishnu, "accept this divine rice and milk, and share it amongst your wives."

Then Dasharatha, overjoyed, carried the divine food and gave a portion of it to Kaushalya, his first wife, and another portion to Sumitra, his second wife, and another to Kaikey, his third wife, and then the fourth portion to Sumitra again. In due time four sons were born to them, sharing the self of Vishnu—from Kaushalya, Rama; from Kaikeyi, Bharata; and from Sumitra, Lakshman and Satrughna.

Meanwhile the gods created mighty monkey-hosts, brave and wise and swift, shape-shifters, hardly to be slain, to be the helpers of the heroic Vishnu in the battle with the rakshasas.

The four sons of Dasharatha grew up to early manhood, excelling all in bravery and virtue. Rama especially became the idol of the people and the favourite of his father. Learned in the arts, he was no less expert in the science of elephants. Lakshman devoted himself to his brother Rama's service, so that the two were together always. Like a faithful shadow Lakshman followed Rama, sharing with him everything that was his own, and guarding him when he went abroad to exercise or hunt. So it was until Rama reached the age of sixteen.

III

Now a priest came to Rama and told him that Janaka, Raja of Mithila, was about to celebrate a great sacrifice.

"Thither," he said, "we shall repair. And you, O tiger among men, shall go with us, and there behold a wonderful and marvellous bow. This great bow the gods gave long ago to Janaka's ancestors; and neither gods nor gandharvas nor asuras nor rakshasas nor men have might to string it, though kings and princes have tried. That bow is worshipped as a god. The bow and Janaka's great sacrifice you shall behold."

So they set out for Janaka's palace. A cool breeze, delighted at the sight of Rama, fanned their faces, and flowers rained down upon them from the sky. The two brothers, carrying their swords, wearing splendid jewels and gloves of lizard skin upon their fingers, followed the priest like glorious flames, making him bright with the reflection of their own radiance.

Janaka welcomed them with much honour, and appointed them to seats according to their rank. He asked the priest who those brothers might be that walked amongst men like lions or elephants, godlike and goodly to be seen.

Next day Janaka summoned the brothers to see the bow. First he told them how that bow had been given by the gods, then he said: "I have a daughter, Sita, not born of men, but sprung from the furrow as I ploughed the field and hallowed it. On him who bends the bow I will bestow my daughter. Kings and princes have tried and failed to bend it. Now I shall reveal the bow to you, and if Rama bends it, I shall give him my daughter Sita."

Then the great bow was brought forth upon an eight-

wheeled cart drawn by five thousand tall men. Rama took
the bow from its case and strove to bend it. It yielded
easily, and he strung and drew it till at last it snapped in
two with the sound of an earthquake or a thunder clap.

Then Janaka praised Rama and gave orders for the
marriage to be prepared, and sent messengers to the city of
Ayodhya to invite Dasharatha to his son's wedding, to give
his blessing and consent.

Thereafter the two kings met, and Janaka bestowed Sita
upon Rama, and his second daughter on Lakshman. And
wives were found for the other brothers, and having thus
won honour, wealth and noble brides, those four best of
men dwelt at Ayodhya, serving their father.

IV

So it passed for a while, until one of Dasharatha's wives
grew jealous of the love that all people gave to Rama, and
she plotted discord. Then Rama went into exile with his
wife Sita and his brother Lakshman, and they dwelt in the
forest, for Rama would not allow himself to be a cause of
strife. They lived as paupers in a dark hut, but the light of
the two brothers which shone from their brows made the
hut more joyous for Sita than marble or silks or fountains
or peacocks. And they journeyed through the forest for
ten years, doing good, and quelling evil where they found
it.

At last they found a green lawn beside a river, whose
waters swarmed with fowl, throngs of deer lived on its
banks, and the hills were covered with good trees and
flowers and herbs. There Lakshman built a spacious bam-
boo house, well thatched with leaves and with a well-

smoothed floor. Thither the giant vulture Jatayu came and pledged friendship; and Rama, Sita and Lakshman were contented, like the gods in heaven.

Now Rama was with Sita, talking to Lakshman, when there came by a fearful and hideous demon, the sister of Ravana, that terrible rakshasa for whose destruction the great God Vishnu had made himself be born. When she saw Rama, the she-demon desired him; but he refused her. She turned to Lakshman; but he would not speak to her. In fury and jealousy, the demon sprang at Sita, but Lakshman took his sword and cut off the foul nose and ears, and she fled away bleeding, till she met another demon brother of hers.

This demon's anger at his sister's maiming was like hailstones, and he sent fourteen rakshasas to slay Rama and Lakshman and Sita, and to bring their blood for his sister to drink. But Rama slew all fourteen with his arrows.

Then the demon was indeed furious, and set out himself with fourteen thousand rakshasas, every one shape-shifters, horrible, proud as lions, big of mouth, courageous, delighting in cruelty.

As this host drove on, many evil omens befell; but the host was blind to defeat, and not to be turned aside from what seemed a small matter—to slay two men and a woman.

Rama, perceiving the oncoming host, sent Lakshman with Sita to a secret cave, and cast on his mail, for he would fight alone; and all the gods and spirits of the air and creatures of heaven came to behold the battle.

The rakshasas drove on like a sea, or heavy clouds, and showered their weapons upon Rama, so that the wood-gods were afraid and fled away. But Rama was not afraid, and troubled the rakshasas with his marrow-piercing shafts, so that they fled to their captain for protection. He rallied them, and they came on again, discharging volleys of uprooted trees and boulders.

It was in vain; for Rama, alone and fighting on foot, slew all the fourteen thousand terrible rakshasas and stood face to face with the leader himself.

A dreadful battle was theirs, as if between a lion and an elephant; the air was dark with flying shafts. At last a fiery arrow, discharged by Rama, consumed the demon. Then the gods, well pleased, showered blossoms upon Rama, and departed. And Sita and Lakshman came forth from the cave.

V

But news of the destruction of the rakshasas was brought to the great Ravana, and he who brought the news advised Ravana to vanquish Rama by carrying Sita away. Ravana approved this plan, and sought out the crafty rakshasa Maricha to further his ends. But Maricha advised Ravana to stay his hand from attempting the impossible, and Ravana, being persuaded for that time, went home to his fortress of Lanka.

Twenty arms and ten heads had Ravana: he sat on his golden throne like a flaming fire fed with sacrificial offerings. He was scarred with the marks of many wounds received in battle with the gods; of royal mien and gorgeously apparelled was that puissant and cruel rakshasa.

His wont was to destroy the sacrifices of holy men and to possess the wives of others—not to be slain by gods or ghosts or birds or serpents. Yet when his sister came to him without nose or ears, and told him of Rama and Sita, and

taunted him for unkingly ways in that he took no revenge
for the slaughter of his subjects and his brother, and when
this demon urged him to bring away Sita and make her his
wife, he took his chariot and fared along by the sea to a
great forest to consult again with the crafty Maricha.

Maricha counselled Ravana not to meddle with Rama.

"You would get off easily," he said, "if Rama, once
angered, left a single rakshasa alive, or held his hand from
destroying the city fortress of Lanka."

But Ravana was vainglorious, and boasted that Rama
would be an easy prey. He blamed Maricha for ill-will
towards himself, and threatened him with death. Then
Maricha out of fear consented, though he looked for no
less than death from Rama when they should meet again.
Then Ravana was pleased, and, taking Maricha in his
chariot, set out for Rama's hermitage, explaining how Sita
should be stolen by a ruse.

Maricha, obedient to Ravana, assumed the form of a
golden deer and ranged about the wood near Rama's
house: its horns were like twin jewels, its face was piebald,
its ears like two blue lotus flowers, its sleek sides soft as the
petals of a flower, its hoofs as black as jet, its haunches
slender, its lifted tail of every colour from the rainbow—a
deer-form such as this he took! His back was starred with
gold and silver, and he ranged about the forest lawns to be
noticed by Sita.

And when she saw him she was astonished and delighted,
and called to Rama and Lakshman, and begged Rama to
catch or kill the deer for her, and she urged him to the chase.
Rama too was fascinated by the splendid deer. He would
not heed Lakshman's warning that it must be a rakshasa
disguised.

"All the more, then, must I slay it," said Rama, "but do

you watch over Sita, staying here with the good vulture Jatayu. I shall be back again in a very little while, bringing the deer-skin with me."

Now vanishing, now coming near, the magic beast led Rama far away, until he was wearied out and sank upon the ground under a shady tree; then it appeared again, surrounded by other deer, and bounded away. But Rama drew his bow and loosed an arrow that pierced its breast, so that it sprang high into the air and fell moaning on the earth.

Then Maricha, on the point of death, assumed his own

shape, and remembering Ravana's command, he bethought him how to draw Lakshman away from Sita, and he called aloud with Rama's voice, "Ah, Sita! Ah, Lakshman!!"

At the sound of that awful cry Rama was struck with nameless fear, and hurried back to his house by the river, leaving Maricha dead.

Now Sita heard that cry, and urged Lakshman to go to Rama's help, upbraiding him with bitter words; for he knew Rama to be unconquerable, and himself was pledged to guard Sita from all danger.

But she called him a monster of wickedness, and said that he cared nothing for Rama, but desired herself; and he might not endure those words, and though many an ill omen warned him, she forced him to go in search of Rama. So he bowed to her and went away, but often turning back to glance at Sita, fearing for her safety.

Now Ravana assumed the shape of a wandering man; carrying a staff and a beggar's bowl, he came towards Sita waiting all alone for Rama to come back. The forest knew him: the very trees stayed still, the wind dropped, the river flowed more slowly for fear. But he came close to Sita, and gazed upon her, and was filled with evil longings; and he addressed her, praising her beauty, and asked her to leave that dangerous forest and go with him to dwell in palaces and gardens.

But she, thinking him a holy man and her guest, gave him food and water, and answered that she was Rama's wife, and told the story of their love; and she asked his name and kin. Then he named his name Ravana, and besought her to be his wife, and offered her palaces, and servants and gardens. But she grew angry, and answered him.

"I am the servant of Rama," said Sita, "lion amongst

men, immovable as any mountain, vast as the mighty ocean. Would you draw the teeth from a lion's mouth, or swim the sea with a heavy stone about your neck? As well might you seek Sun or Moon as me! Little like is Rama unto you, but different as is a lion from a jackal, an elephant from a cat, the ocean from a tiny stream, or gold from iron. If you take me, the wife of Rama, your death is certain, and I shall surely die."

And she shook with fear, as a plantain tree is shaken by the wind.

But Ravana's yellow eyes grew red with anger and the peaceful face changed, and he took his own horrid shape, ten-faced, and twenty-armed; he seized that gentle thing by the hair and limbs, and sprang into his golden ass-drawn chariot, and rose up into the sky. But she cried aloud to Lakshman and to Rama.

"And O you forest and flowery trees," she cried, "and you, our river, and woodland gods, and deer, and birds, I conjure you to tell my lord that Ravana has stolen me away."

Then she saw the great vulture Jatayu on a tree, and prayed him for help. He woke from sleep and, seeing Ravana and Sita, spoke soft words to the rakshasa, advising him to leave his evil course.

"Rama will avenge the wrong with death," said Jatayu, "and while I live you shall not take away the virtuous Sita, but I shall fight with you and fling you from your chariot."

Then Ravana, with angry eyes, sprang upon Jatayu, and there was a deadly battle in the sky; many weapons he showered on Jatayu, while the king of birds wounded Ravana with beak and claw. So many arrows pierced Jatayu that he seemed like a bird half hidden in a nest; but

he broke with his feet two bows of Ravana's, and destroyed the sky-faring chariot, so that Ravana fell down on to the earth, with Sita in his lap.

But Jatayu by then was weary, and Ravana sprang up again and fell upon him, and with a dagger cut away his wings, so that he fell at the point of death. Sita went to her friend, and clasped him with her arms, but he lay motionless and silent like an extinguished forest fire.

Then Ravana seized her again and went his way across the sky. Against the body of the rakshasa she shone like golden lightning amidst heavy clouds, or cloth of gold upon a sable elephant. All nature grieved for her: the lotus flower faded, the sun grew dark, the mountains wept in waterfalls and lifted up their summits like arms, the woodland gods were terrified, the young fawns shed tears, and every creature lamented.

But Brahma, seeing Sita carried away, rejoiced in Heaven, that One Creator of the World, and said, "Our work is accomplished now," forseeing Ravana's death. The hermits were glad and sorry at once: sorry for Sita, and glad that Ravana must die.

Now, as they drove through the sky in such a fashion, Sita saw five great monkeys on a mountain top, and to them she cast down her jewels and her golden veil as a token for Rama.

Ravana left behind the woods and mountains, and crossed the sea, and came to his great fortress city of Lanka, and put Sita in an inner room, all alone and served and guarded well. Spies were sent to keep watch on Rama. Then Ravana returned and showed to Sita all his palace and treasure and gardens, and prayed her to be his wife, and wooed her in every way; but she hid her face and sobbed with wordless tears.

And when he urged her again she took a blade of grass and laid it between Ravana and herself, and prophesied his death at Rama's hands and the ruin of all rakshasas, and utterly rejected him. Then he turned from prayer to threats, and, calling horrid rakshasas, gave her to their charge, and commanded them to break her spirit, whether by violence or by temptation. There was the gentle Sita, like a sinking ship, or a doe amongst a pack of dogs.

2. HANUMAN

VI

Now Rama, returning from the chase of Maricha, was heavy-hearted, and meeting Lakshman, he blamed him much for leaving Sita.

The jackals howled and birds cried as they hurried back. Near to the house the feet of Rama failed him, and a trembling shook his frame; for Sita was not there.

They ranged the groves of flowering trees, and the river banks where lotus flowers were open, and sought the mountain caves, and asked the river and the trees and all the animals where Sita was. Then Rama deemed that rakshasas had eaten her, taking revenge for the first battle. But next they came to where Jatayu had fought with Ravana, and saw the broken weapons and the chariot and the trampled ground; and Rama raged against all beings, and would destroy the very heavens and earth, unless the gods gave back his Sita.

Then they noticed the dying Jatayu, and deeming him to be a rakshasa that had eaten Sita, Rama was about to slay him. But Jatayu spoke feebly, and related to Rama all that had befallen, so that Rama, throwing down his bow, embraced the bird and lamented for his death; and Jatayu told of Ravana and comforted Rama with assurances of victory and recovery of Sita. But therewith his spirit fled away, and his head and body sank down upon the ground; and Rama mourned over his friend.

"Ah, Lakshman," he said, "this kingly bird dwelt here contented many years, and now is dead because of me: he has given up his life in trying to rescue Sita. Behold, amongst the animals of every rank there are heroes, even amongst birds. I am more sorry for this vulture that has died for me than even because of Sita's loss."

Then Lakshman brought wood and fire, and they burned Jatayu there with every rite and offering due, and spoke the prayers for his speedy coming to the abodes of the shining gods; and that king of vultures, slain in battle for a good cause, and blessed by Rama, attained a glorious state.

Then Rama and Lakshman set out to search for Sita far and wide; it was but a little time before they met a horrid rakshasa, and it was no light matter for them to come to their above in battle with him. But he, wounded to death, rejoiced, for he had been cursed with that form by a hermit until Rama should slay and set him free. Rama and Lakshman burnt him on a mighty pyre, and he rose from it, and, mounting upon a heavenly chariot, he spoke to Rama, counselling him to seek the help of the great monkey Sugriva and the four other monkeys that dwelt on the mountain.

"Do not despise that royal monkey," he said, "for he is puissant, humble, brave, expert, and graceful, good at shifting shapes, and well acquainted with the haunts of every rakshasa. Do you make alliance with him, taking a vow of friendship before a fire as witness, and with his help you will surely win back Sita."

Then he departed, bidding them farewell and pointing the way to the mountain; and they came to that wooded mountain, place of many birds, beside the Pampa lake.

Now this monkey Sugriva lived in exile, driven from home and robbed of his wife by his cruel brother; and when he saw the great-eyed heroes bearing arms, he deemed them to have been sent by his brother for his destruction.

So he fled away, and he sent his next monkey, Hanuman, disguised as a hermit, to speak with the heroes and learn their purpose. Then Lakshman told him all that had befallen, and that now Rama sought Sugriva's aid. So Hanuman, considering that Sugriva also needed a champion for the recovery of his wife and kingdom, led the heroes to Sugriva, and there Rama and the monkey-chief held converse.

Hanuman made fire with two pieces of wood, and passing sunwise about it, Rama and Sugriva were made sworn friends, and each bound himself to aid the other. They gazed at each other intently, and neither had his fill of seeing the other. Then Sugriva told his story and prayed Rama for his aid, and he engaged himself to be the monkey-chief's brother, and in return Sugriva undertook to recover Sita.

He told Rama how he had seen her carried away by Ravana, and how she had dropped her veil and her jewels, and he showed these tokens to Rama.

Rama knew them, but Lakshman said, "I do not recognize the bracelets or the ear-rings, but I know the anklets well, for I was not used to lift my eyes above her feet."

Now Rama fared with Sugriva to the monkey-king's city, and overcame the cruel usurper, and established Sugriva on the throne.

Then four months of the rainy season passed away, and when the skies grew clear and the floods diminished, Sugriva sent out his marshals to summon the monkey host. They came from Himalaya and Vindhya and Kailas, from the east and from the west, from far and near, from caves and forests, in hundreds and thousands and millions, and each host was captained by a veteran leader.

All the monkeys in the world assembled there, and

stood before Sugriva with joined hands. Then Sugriva gave them to Rama for his service, and would place them under his command. But Rama thought it best that Sugriva should issue all orders, since he best understood the stratagems of such a host, and was well acquainted with the matter to be accomplished.

VII

As yet, neither Rama nor Lakshman nor Sugriva knew more of Ravana than his name; none could tell how or where he dwelt or where he kept Sita hidden. Sugriva therefore dispatched all the host under leaders to search the four quarters for a month, as far as the uttermost bound of any land where men or demons dwelt or sun shone.

But he trusted as much in Hanuman as in all the host together; for Hanuman, the son of the wind-god, had his father's energy and swiftness and vehemence and power of access to every place in earth or sky, and he was brave and politic and keen of wit and well aware of conduct befitting the time and place. And much as Sugriva relied on Hanuman, Hanuman was even more confident of his own power. Rama also put his trust in Hanuman, and gave him his signet-ring to show for a sign to Sita when he should discover her.

Then Hanuman bowed to Rama's feet, and departed with the host appointed to search the southern quarter, while Rama remained a month with Sugriva, expecting his return.

And after a month the hosts came back from searching the north and west and east, sorry and dejected that they had not found Sita. But the southern host searched all the woods and caves and hidden places, till at last they came to the mighty ocean, boundless, resounding, covered with dreadful waves. A month had passed and Sita was not found, therefore the monkeys sat, gazing over the sea and waiting for their end, for they dared not return to Sugriva.

But there dwelt a mighty and very aged vulture in a neighbouring cave, and he, hearing the monkeys talking of his brother Jatayu, came forth and asked for news of him. Then the monkeys related to him the whole affair, and the vulture answered that he had seen Sita carried away by Ravana and that Ravana dwelt in Lanka, a hundred leagues across the sea.

"Do you repair thither," he said, "and avenge the rape of Sita and the murder of my brother. For I have the gift of foresight, and even now I perceive that Ravana and Sita are there in Lanka."

Then the monkeys grew more hopeful, but when they marched down to the shore and sat beside the heaving sea they were again downcast, and took counsel together sadly enough.

Now one monkey said he could bound over twenty leagues, and another fifty, and one eighty, and one ninety; and one could cross over a hundred, but his power would not avail for the return. Then a noble monkey addressed Hanuman, and recalled his birth and origin, how the wind-god had begotten him and his mother had reared him in the mountains, and when he was still a child he had thought the sun to be a fruit growing in the sky, and sprang easily three thousand leagues towards it.

"And do you, heroic monkey, prove your prowess now and bound across the ocean," he said, "for we look on you as our champion, and you do surpass all things in movement and in vehemence."

L

Then Hanuman roused himself, and the monkey host rejoiced. Swelling with pride and might, he boasted of the deed he would accomplish.

Then he rushed up the mountain Mahendra, shaking it in his wrath and frightening every beast that lived in its woods and caves. Intent upon achieving a hard task, where no friend could help and no foe hindered, Hanuman stood with head uplifted like a bull, praying to the sun, to the mountain wind and to all beings, he set his heart in the work to be accomplished.

He grew great, and stood, like a fire, with bristling hair, and roared like thunder, brandishing his tail; so he gathered energy of mind and body.

"I will discover Sita or bring Ravana away in chains," he thought, and therewith sprang up so that the very trees were dragged after him with his force. He hurtled through the air, his flashing eyes like forest fires, his lifted tail like the rainbow.

So Hanuman held his way across the ocean. Nor, when the friendly ocean lifted up Mount Mainaka, well wooded and full of fruits and roots, would Hanuman stay to rest, but, rising up, coursed through the shining air.

Then a grim she-demon rose from the sea and caught him by the shadow, and would devour him, but he dashed into her mouth, and, growing exceeding great, burst away again, leaving her dead and broken. Then he perceived the farther shore, and thinking his huge form ill-fitted for a secret mission, he resumed his natural size and shape, and so alighted on the shore of Lanka, nor was he ever so wearied or fatigued.

On the mountain summit Hanuman beheld the city of Lanka, girt with a golden wall, and filled with buildings huge as cloudy mountains. Impatiently he waited for the setting of the sun; then, shrinking to the size of a cat, he entered the city at night, unseen by the guards.

Hanuman made his way to the palace of Ravana, towering on the mountain top, girt with wall and moat. By now the moon was full and high, sailing like a swan, and Hanuman beheld the dwellers in the palace, some drinking, some sorry and some glad, some eating, some making music, and some sleeping. Many a fair bride lay in her husband's arms, but Sita of peerless virtue he could not find; wherefore that eloquent monkey was cast down and disappointed.

Then he sprang from court to court, visiting the quarters of all the foremost rakshasas, till at last he came to Ravana's own apartments, a very mine of gold and jewels, ablaze with silver light. Everywhere he sought for Sita, and left no corner unexplored; golden stairs and painted chariots and crystal windows and secret chambers set with gems, all these he beheld, but never Sita. The odour of meat and drink he sniffed, and to his nostrils there came also the all-pervading Air, and it said to him:

"Come hither, where Ravana lies."

Following Air, he came to Ravana's sleeping place. There lay the lord of the rakshasas upon a glorious bed asleep and breathing heavily. Huge was his frame, decked with splendid jewels, like a crimson sunset cloud pierced by flashes of lightning; his big hands lay on the white cloth like terrible five-hooded serpents. Four golden lamps on pillars lit his bed.

Around him lay his wives, fair as the moon, decked in glorious gems and garlands that never faded. And there was Ravana's queen, exceeding all other in her splendour and loveliness; and Hanuman guessed she must be Sita, and the thought enlivened him, so that he waved his arms and frisked his tail and sang and danced and climbed the golden pillars and sprang down again, as his monkey-nature moved him.

But reflection showed his error, for he said: "Without Rama, Sita would not eat or drink or sleep or decorate her person, nor would she company with any other than he. This is some other one."

So Hanuman ranged farther through the palace, searching many a bower in vain. Many fair ones he beheld, but never Sita, and he deemed she must be slain or eaten by the rakshasas. So he left the palace and sat awhile in deep dejection on the city wall.

"If I return without discovering Sita," he reflected, "my labour will have been in vain. And what will my king Sugriva say, and Rama, and the monkey host? Surely Rama will die of grief. No more shall the noble monkeys assemble amongst the woods and mountains or in secret places and indulge in games; but a loud wailing will arise when I return, and they will swallow poison, or hang themselves, or jump down from lofty mountains. Therefore I must not return unsuccessful; better that I should starve and die. It is not right that all those noble monkeys should perish on my account. I shall remain here and search Lanka again and again; even this Asoka wood beyond the walls shall be examined."

Then Hanuman bowed to Rama, to Sita, and to Death; to the Wind, the Moon and Fire, and to Sugriva, and praying to these with thought intent, he ranged the Asoka wood with his imagination—and met with Sita. Then he sprang from the wall like an arrow from a bow, and entered the wood in bodily shape.

The wood was a place of pleasure and delight, full of

flowering trees and happy animals; but Hanuman ravaged
it and broke the trees.

One beautiful Asoka tree stood alone, amongst pavilions
and gardens, built round with golden pavements and
silver walls. Hanuman sprang up this tree and kept watch
all about, thinking that Sita, if she were in the forest, would
come to that lovely place. He saw a marble palace, with
stairs of coral and floors of shining gold, and there lay one
imprisoned, weak and thin as if with fasting, sighing for
heavy grief, clad in soiled robes, and guarded by horrid
demons, like a deer among the dogs or a shining flame
behind smoke.

Then Hanuman considered that this must be Sita, for
she was fair and spotless, like a moon overcast by clouds,
and she wore such jewels as Rama had described to him.
Hanuman shed tears of joy and thought of Rama and
Lakshman. But now, while he was yet hidden on the tree,
Ravana had waked, and that lordly rakshasa came with a
great train of women to the Asoka wood, and Hanuman
heard the sound of their tinkling anklets as they passed
across the golden pavements.

Ravana came toward Sita, and when she saw him she
trembled like a plantain tree shaken by the wind, and hid
her face and sobbed. Then he wooed her in every way,
tempting her with wealth and power and comfort; but she
refused him utterly, and foretold his death at Rama's hands.

But Ravana waxed wood-wrath, and gave a two month
term, after which, if she yielded not, she should be tor-
tured and slain; and leaving her to the horrid guards with
orders to break her will, Ravana returned with his wives to
his apartment. Then Sita crept to the foot of the Asoka
tree where Hanuman was hidden.

Hanuman reflected that there was need for him to

speak with Sita; but he feared to frighten her, or to attract the notice of the guard and bring destruction on himself, for, though he had might to slay the rakshasa host, he could not, if wearied out, return across the ocean.

So he stayed hidden in the branches of the tree and recited Rama's virtues and deeds, speaking in gentle tones, till Sita heard him. She caught her breath with fear and looked up into the tree, and saw the monkey; eloquent was he and humble, and his eyes glowed like golden fire. Then he came down out of the tree, and with joined palms spoke to Sita. Then she told him that she was Sita and asked for news of Rama, and Hanuman told her all that had befallen and spoke of Rama and Lakshman, so that she was well-nigh as glad as if she had seen Rama himself.

But Hanuman came a little nearer, and Sita was much afraid, thinking him to be Ravana in disguise. He had much ado to persuade her that he was Rama's friend. But at last, when she beheld the signet-ring, it seemed to her as if she were already saved, and she was glad and sorry at once— glad to know that Rama was alive and well, and sorry for his grief.

Then Hanuman suggested that he should carry Sita on his back across the sea to Rama. She praised his strength, but would not go with him, because she thought she might fall from his back into the sea, especially if the rakshasas followed them, and because she would not willingly touch any person but Rama, and because she desired that the glory of her rescue and the destruction of the rakshasas should be Rama's.

"But do you speedily bring Rama here," she prayed.

Then Hanuman praised her wisdom and modesty, and asked for a token for Rama; and she told him of an adventure with a crow, known only to herself and Rama, and she gave him a jewel from her hair, and sent a message to Rama and to Lakshman, praying them to rescue her.

Hanuman took the gem and, bowing to Sita, made ready to depart. Then Sita gave him another message, by which Rama might surely know that Hanuman had found her.

"Tell him, 'One day my brow spot was wiped away, and you did paint another with red earth. And, O Rama, do you come soon, for ten months have passed already since I saw you, and I may not endure more than another month'. And good fortune go with you, heroic monkey," she said.

But Hanuman was not satisfied with finding Sita. He dashed about the Asoka wood and broke the trees and spoiled the pavilions, like the Wind himself.

The demons sent messages to Ravana for help, saying that a mighty monkey was destroying his servants, and Ravana ordered a mighty rakshasa, bow in hand, to slay

Hanuman forthwith. And indeed he wounded him with a sharp arrow as he sat upon a temple roof, but Hanuman hurled a bolt at him and crushed him utterly.

Then a host of heroic rakshasas proceeded against Hanuman and met their death. And another great demon came, and sent a million shafts against the monkey, but he, ranging the sky, escaped them all. Then the demon paused, and with concentrated mind pondered over the true nature of Hanuman, and with spiritual insight perceived that he was not to be slain by weapons.

Therefore he devised a way to bind him, and therewith Hanuman was bound, and knew the bond unbreakable, and he fell to earth. But he reflected that it would be well for him to converse with Ravana, and so he struggled not, but let the rakshasas bear him off.

But they, seeing him still, bound him yet closer with cords and bark. But that binding was the means of his release, for the power of the demon's thought-bond was broken as soon as an earthly binding was added to it.

Yet the wily monkey gave no sign that the ties were loosed, and the fierce rakshasas, crying to each other, "Who is he? What does he want?" and, "Kill him! Burn him! Eat him!" dragged him before Ravana.

Questioned by Ravana's minister, Hanuman answered that he was indeed a monkey, come to Lanka as Rama's envoy to accomplish his commands and to behold Ravana. And he told the story of Rama up till then, and gave Ravana sound advice, to save his life by surrendering Sita.

Ravana was furious and would have Hanuman slain, but the counsellors reminded him that the punishment of death could not justly be inflicted upon one who named himself an envoy. So Ravana cast about for a fitting penalty, and bethought him to set Hanuman's tail afire.

Then the rakshasas bound the monkey's tail with cotton soaked in oil and set it ablaze. But the heroic monkey cherished a secret plan. He suffered the rakshasas to lead him about Lanka that he might better learn its ways and strength.

Word was taken to Sita that the monkey with whom she had conversed was led about the streets of Lanka and proclaimed a spy, and that his tail was burning. Thereat she grieved, and praying to Fire, she said: "As I have been faithful to my lord, do you be cool to Hanuman."

Fire flamed up in answer to her prayer, and at that very moment Hanuman's sire, Wind, blew cool between the flame and Hanuman.

Perceiving that the fire still burnt, but that his tail was ice-cold, Hanuman thought that it was for Rama's sake and Sita's that the fire was chilled and he snapped his bonds and sprang into the sky, and rushed to and fro in Lanka, burning the palaces and all their treasures. And when he had burnt half Lanka to the ground and slaughtered many a rakshasa, Hanuman quenched his tail in the sea.

Then at once he repented of his rash deed, and thought that Sita must have died in the fire.

"It is small matter," he said, "to have burnt Lanka. But if Sita has lost her life I have failed altogether in my work, and will rather die than return in vain to Rama." But again he said, "It may be that that fair one has been saved by her own virtue. The fire that scorched me not has surely never hurt that noble lady."

Therewith he hastened back to the Asoka wood and found her seated there, and he greeted her, and she him, and once more they spoke of Rama, and Hanuman foretold that he would speedily rescue Sita and slay the rakshasas.

Then Hanuman sprang up like a winged mountain and fared across the sea, now clearly seen, now hidden by the clouds, till he came to the mountain Mahendra, flourishing his tail and roaring like the wind in a mighty cavern. And all the monkeys rejoiced exceedingly to see and hear him, knowing that he must have found Sita. They danced, and ran from peak to peak, and waved the branches of trees and their clean white cloths, and brought fruits and roots for Hanuman to eat. Then Hanuman reported all that he had done, while the monkey host sat round about him there on Mahendra's summit.

When all had been told, that monkey host, the searchers of the southern quarter, cried, "Our work is done, and the time has come to return to our king Sugriva. Let us go." Then Hanuman leapt up into the air, followed by all the monkeys, darkening the sky as if with clouds and roaring, and coming speedily to Sugriva, they spoke first to the heavy-hearted Rama and gave him tidings of Sita, and praised the work of Hanuman.

Then Rama talked with Hanuman, and asked him many a question, and Hanuman told him all, and showed him the jewel and gave him Sita's words.

Next, Sugriva spoke and issued orders for a march of all the host toward the far south to lay a siege to Lanka, while Hanuman reported to Rama all that he had learnt of the strength and fortifications of the city, saying:

"Do you regard the city as already taken, for I alone have laid it waste, and it will be an easy matter for such a host as this to destroy it utterly."

Now the monkey host went on its way, led by Sugriva and Rama, and the monkeys skipped for joy and bounded gleefully and sported one with another. With them went many friendly bears, guarding the rear.

Passing over many mountains and delightful forests, the army came at length to Mahendra, and beheld the deep sea before them. Thence they marched to the very shore, beside the wave-washed rocks, and made their camp. They covered all the shore, like a second sea beside the tossing waves.

Then Rama summoned a council to devise a means for crossing over the ocean, and a guard was set, and orders issued that none should wander, for he feared the magic of the rakshasas.

3. THE SIEGE OF LANKA

VIII

Meanwhile Ravana in Lanka called another council.

"You know how the monkey Hanuman harried Lanka, and now Rama has reached the ocean shore with a host of bears and monkeys, and he will dry the sea or bridge it and besiege us here. Do you consider the means of protection for the city and the army."

Thus spoke Ravana to his counsellors. And his generals advised him to entrust the battle to his son, Prince Indrajit, while others, the great leaders, boasted that they alone would swallow up the monkey army. But Vibhishana, the younger brother of Ravana, advised another course.

"Force," said he, "is only to be resorted to when other means fail—conciliation, gifts, and sowing of dissension. Moreover, force avails only against such as are weak or are displeasing to the gods. What but death can result from a conflict with Rama, self-controlled and vigilant and strong with the might of all the gods? Who ever thought that Hanuman should have done so much? And from this you should be warned and yield up Sita to her lord, to save yourself and us."

And playing a perilous part, he followed Ravana his brother to his own chamber and saluted him, and spoke yet further for his welfare.

"From the day that Sita came," he said, "the omens have been evil: fire is ever obscured by smoke, serpents are found in kitchens, the milk of cows runs dry, wild beasts howl around the palace. Do you restore Sita, lest we all suffer for your sin."

But Ravana dismissed his brother angrily, and boasted that he would hold Sita as his own, even if all the gods should war against him.

Therefore he took counsel again with his generals of war, but again his brother opposed him, till Ravana cursed him angrily as a coward and a traitor. Then the brother deemed it the time when he should suffer no more of these insults, and rising into the air, he said to Ravana:

"I spoke for your welfare: now fare you well."

So saying, he passed through the sky across the sea and came to the monkey host, and announced himself as come to make alliance with Rama. Most of the monkey leaders were for slaying him, for they put little faith in a rakshasa, but Rama spoke him fair, and engaged, in return for his help in the war, to set him on the throne of Lanka when Ravana should have been slain.

They had now to find a way to cross the water. And Rama, spreading a couch of sacrificial grass, lay down upon it, facing the east, with praying hands toward the sea, resolving that either the ocean should yield or he would die.

Thus Rama lay three days, silent, concentred, following the rule, intent upon the ocean. But Ocean answered not.

Then Rama was angered, and rose and took his bow, and would dry up the sea and lay fish bare; and he loosed dreadful shafts that flamed and pierced the waters, awakening mighty storms, so that the god-hermits haunting the sky cried out, "Alas!" and "Enough!" But Ocean did not show himself, and Rama, threatening him, set to his bow an arrow blessed with a charm, and drew.

Then heaven and earth were darkened and the mountains trembled, lightnings flashed, and every creature was afraid, and the mighty deep was wrought with violent movement.

Then Ocean himself rose from the water like the sun. Jewelled and wreathed was he and decked with many gems, and followed by noble rivers. He came to Rama with joined palms and spoke him fair.

"O Rama," said he, "you know that every element has its own quality. Mine is this, to be fathomless and hard to cross. Neither for love nor fear can I stay the waters from their endless movement. But you shall pass over me by means of a bridge, and I will suffer it and hold it firm."

Then Rama was appeased, but the charmed arrow he held waited to find its mark, and would not be restrained.

"Where may I let this arrow strike?" said Rama.

"There is a part of my domain toward the north, haunted by evil wights," said Ocean. "There let it fall."

Rama let fly the flaming shaft, and the water of the sea toward the north was dried and burnt, and where the sea had been became a desert. But Rama blessed the desert, and made it fruitful.

Ocean said to Rama, "O kind one, there is a monkey here named Nala. Full of energy he is, and he shall build

the bridge across me, and I shall bear it up." Then Ocean
sank beneath the waters.

But Nala said to Rama, "Ocean has spoken truth: only
because you did not ask me I hid my power till now."

All the monkeys, following Nala's orders, gathered trees
and rocks, and brought them from the forests to the shore,
and set them in the sea. Some carried timber, some used
the measuring rods, some bore stones; huge was the tumult
and noise of crags thrown into the sea.

The first day fourteen leagues were made, and on the
fifth day the bridge was finished, broad and elegant and
firm—like a line of parting of the hair on Ocean's head.

Then the monkey host passed over, Rama and Lakshman
riding on their backs. Some monkeys went along the
causeway, others plunged into the sea, and others coursed
through the air, and the noise of them drowned the beat of
the ocean waves.

Dreadful were the omens of war that showed themselves:
the earth shook, the clouds rained blood, a fiery circle fell
from the sun. But the monkeys roared defiance at the
rakshasas, whose destruction was thus foretold.

Then Rama, beholding Lanka towering up to pierce the
heavens, wrought, as it were, of mind rather than of
substance, hanging in the sky like a bank of snow-white
clouds, was downcast at the thought of Sita prisoned there.
But he arrayed the host of bears and monkeys, and laid
siege to Lanka.

IX

Meanwhile Ravana's spies, sent in monkey shape to
gather news, brought tidings thereof to Lanka, and, advising their master of Rama's power, counselled that Sita

should be surrendered. But Ravana was enraged, and drove the spies away disgraced, and sent others in their place, but ever with the same result.

No help was there, then, but to give battle or to yield up Rama's bride, yet Ravana sought first to betray Sita to his will.

He told her that Rama was slain, the monkey host dispersed, and a she-demon came in, bringing the semblance of Rama's head and bow, and Sita knew them, and was grieving out of all measure, and crying aloud with many lamentations, and she prayed Ravana to slay her by Rama's head that she might follow him. But therewith came in a messenger from the rakshasa general calling Ravana to the battle, and he turned to the field of war. And when he left, the head and bow immediately vanished, and Sita knew them to have been but counterfeits and vain illusions.

Now the monkeys advanced upon Lanka, and swarmed about the walls, flooding the moat and striking terror in the hearts of the rakshasas. Scaling parties climbed the walls and battered down the gates with trees and stones. The rakshasas sallied forth in turn with horrid trumpetings and joined in battle with the monkeys, and all the air was filled with the noise of fighting, and terrible confusion arose of friend and foe and man and beast, and the earth was strewn with flesh.

Thus an equal battle was fought till evening, but the rakshasas waited for the night, and eagerly desired the setting of the sun, for dark is the rakshasa's time of strength. So night fell, and the demons ranged, devouring monkeys by thousands.

Then the monkey chiefs began to roar and frisked their tails. Drums and kettledrums were struck, and seizing trees, the monkeys advanced again on the gates of Lanka.

The rangers of the night issued forth from Lanka under the rakshasa Greyeye, and there was a deadly onset. The monkeys bit and tore and fought with trees and stones, and the rakshasas killed and wounded them with arrows and cleft them with axes and crushed them with maces.

Then seeing the monkeys hard pressed, Hanuman laid about him lustily, and armed with a mountain-top, he

rushed on Greyeye. But the rakshasa brought down his mace on Hanuman and wounded him sore; then Hanuman heedless of the hurt, let fly the mountain-top and crushed the rakshasa to the ground. Seeing their leader slain, the others fled.

Short was the peace ere Ravana sent out other leaders of demons. He sent out Longhand and Manslayer and Noisy-throat and Tall. That encounter was the death of many hundred rakshasas and monkeys, but at last the rakshasas drew back; like water rushing through a broken dyke they melted away and entered Lanka.

But soon came Bigbelly and Threeheads, fighters with mountains and flaming maces; and the Prince Indrajit, the son of Ravana, came riding on a chariot with a magic figure of Sita, and he rode up and down the field, holding her by the hair and striking her, and he cut her down in the sight of all the monkey host. Hanuman, believing in the false show, stayed the battle and brought the news to Rama, and Rama fell down, like a tree cut off at the root.

But Ravana's brother, who had deserted the evil cause, spoke up and said: "It is a device."

Then Rama rose, and Lakshman with him, and took the force of the battle themselves, to come at Prince Indrajit. And it is said that the ancestors and gods, the birds and snakes, protected Lakshman from all shafts so that he could attain his purpose. He took an arrow, and prayed to its indwelling god: "If Rama be the first of all men in heroism, then slay this son of Ravana." And drawing the straight-speeding arrow to his ear he loosed it, and it severed Indrajit from his head, and all the rakshasas, seeing their captain slaughtered, cast down their arms and fled. And all the monkeys rejoiced, for no rakshasa hero remained alive save Ravana himself.

Bitterly Ravana grieved for his son.

"The triple worlds, and this earth with all its forests, seem to me vacant," he cried, "since you, my hero child, have gone to the abode of Yama. You should have performed my funeral rites, not I yours."

And Ravana determined to slay Sita for revenge, but a wise one of his court said, "You may not slay a woman, but when Rama is dead, then shall you possess her."

Ravana went with Bigbelly and Squinteye and Fatflank to the battle, followed by the last of the demon army.

"I shall make an end of Rama and Lakshman," said Ravana.

Nor could the monkeys stand before him, but were destroyed like flies in fire, and therewith both armies joined again, and there was deadly play on either hand, and either army shrank like a pond in summer.

Now Bigbelly and Squinteye and Fatflank were hewn down, but Ravana came on, and scattering the monkeys right and left.

He stayed not ere he came to Rama and Lakshman. He took his way where Rama stood aside, with great eyes like the petals of the lotus, long of arm, unconquerable, holding a bow so huge it seemed to be painted on the sky.

Rama set arrows to the bow and drew the string, so that a thousand rakshasas died of terror when they heard it twang; and there began a deadly battle between the foes.

Those arrows pierced Ravana like hooded snakes, and fell hissing to the ground, but Ravana lifted up a dreadful asura weapon, and let fly at Rama a shower of arrows having the faces of lions and tigers, and some with gaping mouths like wolves. Rama answered these with shafts faced like the sun and stars, like meteors or lightning flashes, destroying the shafts of Ravana.

Then Ravana fought with a rudra shaft, irresistible and flaming, hung with eight noisy bells. It struck Lakshman, and he fell, nor could any monkey draw the shaft out of him. Rama stooped and drew it forth and broke it in twain.

"Now," said Rama, "is the time appointed come at last. Today I shall accomplish a deed of which all men and gods and every world shall tell as long as the earth supports a living creature. Today is my sorrow's end, and all that for which I have laboured shall come to pass."

Then Rama set his mind upon the battle, but Hanuman went to Himalaya and brought the Mount of Healing Herbs for Lakshman, and made Lakshman to smell its savour, so that he rose up whole and well.

Rama mounted upon his chariot, and seemed to light the whole world with his splendour. But Ravana loosed at him a rakshasa weapon, and its golden shafts, with fiery faces vomitting flames, poured over Rama from every side and changed to venomous serpents.

But Rama took a garuda weapon and loosed a flight of golden arrows, changing at will to birds, and devouring all the serpent arrows of the rakshasa.

Then the indwelling gods of all the weapons came to stand by Rama, and Rama hymned the Sun, and purified himself with water-sippings, and was glad; and he turned to deal with Ravana, for the rakshasa had come to himself again and was eager for the battle.

Each like a flaming lion fought the other. Head after head of the many-necked did Rama cut away with his deadly arrows, but new heads ever rose in place of those cut off, and Ravana's death seemed nowise nearer than before.

Then Rama took up a weapon: the Wind lay in its wings, the Sun and Fire in its head. Blessing that shaft, Rama set it to his bow and loosed it, and it sped to its appointed place and cleft the breast of Ravana, and, bathed in blood, returned and entered Rama's quiver humbly.

Thus was the lord of the rakshasas slain, and the gods rained flowers on Rama's chariot and gave thanks, for their desired end was now accomplished—that end for which alone the Great Vishnu had taken human form. The heavens were at peace, the air grew clear and bright, and the sun shone cloudless on the field of battle.

4. VISHNU

X

Hanuman went to the Asoka tree, and there discovered
Sita; and Sita and Rama were rejoined, she bathed and
fitly adorned with sandal-paste and jewels, and he decked
in the blossom from the gods and with the hurts of war
cleansed from him. And thereafter Rama sat on his father's
throne and governed the city of Ayodhya for ten thousand
years, and Sita bore him two sons.

Then one day there blew a sweet, cool, fragrant air, such
as used to blow only in the golden age, and folk were
astonished that the air should blow also in the second age.
And a heavenly throne rose up from within the earth,
borne on the heads of mighty spirits, and Earth stretched
out her arms to Sita, who was first given to her father
from the new turned furrow of the land and had no mortal
mother, and Sita took her place on the throne, and the
throne sank down again.

But Rama sat stricken with grief, and he was torn by
anger that Sita had disappeared before his eyes. But Brahma
spoke, and said:

"O Rama of firm vows, you should not weep. Rather
remember your godhead, and bethink you that you are
Vishnu. You shall be with Sita in Heaven."

But now Rama was heavy-hearted, and the whole world
seemed empty without Sita, and he knew no peace. He
gave the monkeys and the kings and hermits gifts and sent
each back to his own place; and he made a golden image
of Sita to be with him in his loneliness, and a thousand
years passed.

And so Rama's course on earth was run, and he felt godhead stir within him. He said to Hanuman:

"It is determined already that you shall live for ever. Do you be glad on earth so long as the tale of me endures."

And all the people of Ayodhya, with the beasts and birds and the least of breathing things, and the bears and rakshasas and monkeys followed Rama from the city with happy hearts.

When they came to the river, Brahma, the Creator, came with the godly folk and a hundred thousand chariots, and the wind of Heaven blew and flowers rained upon earth. Then Brahma said to Rama:

"Hail, O Vishnu! Do you, with your brothers, enter in again in whatsoever form you will, you who are the refuge of all creatures and beyond the range of thought or speech."

Then Vishnu entered Heaven in his own form, and all the gods bowed down to him and rejoiced.

And Brahma appointed places in the heavens for all those who had come after Rama, and the bears and monkeys assumed their godly forms. Thus did all beings there assembled attain to the heavenly state, and Brahma and the gods returned to their own abode.

Thus ends Ramayana, revered by Brahma and made by Valmiki. He that has no sons shall attain a son by reading even a single verse of Rama's lay. All sin is washed away from those who read or hear it read. He who recites Ramayana should have rich gifts of cows and gold. Long shall he live who reads Ramayana, and shall be honoured, with his sons and grandsons, in this world and in Heaven.

In the Strange Isle

In the strange isle,
In the green freckled wood and grassy glade,
Strangely the man, the panther and the shadow
Move by the well and the white stones.

Voices cry out in trees, and fingers beckon,
The wings of a million butterflies are sunlit eyes,
There is no sword
In the enchanted wood.

Branches bend over like a terror,
The sun is darkened,
The white wind and the sun and the curling wave
Cradle the coral shore and the tall forest.

Ceaseless the struggle in the twining circles,
The gulls, the doves, and the dark crows;
The fangs of the lily bleed, and the lips
Of the rose are torn.

Trees crash at midnight unpredicted,
Voices cry out,
Naked he walks, and with no fear,
In the strange isle, the wise and gentle.

MICHAEL ROBERTS

The Smoker

A BOY lived in the woods, and his father told him never to go eastward, but to play in the clearing by their hut or to walk towards the west.

For some years the boy obeyed his father, but as he grew older and the paths of the west became dusty with use, he felt himself drawn to the unknown trees, and the green trackways, and one day he set off towards the east.

He found a lake, and knelt down to drink, but the water was alive with savage fish and he nearly lost a hand. He crouched by the shore and watched the fins swirl the water, and a stranger came up behind him so softly that the boy knew nothing until the man spoke.

"Let us see who can throw a spear the farthest."

"Very well," said the boy, and he won easily.

"Let us run round the lake," said the man.

"I agree," said the boy, and he won that, too.

"Let me show you the island in the middle of the lake," said the man.

"Do you like fish?" said the boy. "I can see the island from here."

The man whistled, and a boat came into sight, drawn by three flying swans. The man and the boy stepped into the boat, and were carried to the island, but as soon as they landed the boy wished that he had stayed at home, for the man knocked him down, and left him, and went back across the lake.

The boy felt his bruises. Nothing was broken, although he ached from the fists. He limped about the island to find food, but there was little except berries and roots, and no shelter. He sat and watched the night come.

"If you would be good enough to dig an inch or so into the earth," said a voice close by him, "you would do me a great kindness."

The boy was startled, for there was no one to be seen.

"I'm in the leaf mould," said the voice.

The boy scraped the last year's autumn, and underneath he found a skeleton lying yellow on the ground.

"I am much obliged," said the skeleton. "Now one more thing, if you will. Under that tree, just by the bole, there's a pouch buried. Would you bring it to me?"

The boy put his hand down by the bole, and he found a tobacco pouch in the soil and a pipe and flint.

"It would gratify me," said the skeleton, "if you would light the pipe and put it in my mouth."

The boy did so, and held the pipe between the skeleton's teeth.

"Ah, thank you. Thank you," said the skeleton. "It's the mice, you see. They nest in my ribs, and only the smoke will move them. Such a torment they are, and such a blessing this is."

The boy sat without moving until the skeleton had finished the pipe. "Now," said the skeleton, "you will want to know what you can do about the man who brought you here. Well, I'll help you. He's on his way now with dogs, to hunt you for sport, so you must run up and down all over the island, leaving tracks, and be sure to touch every tree. Then, when he comes, hide at the top of a tree, and they will never find you."

And that is what the boy did, and the dogs could not

find him, for his scent was everywhere. At dawn the man took them off and went back to the land.

"He will come at night," said the skeleton, "and it will be to drink your blood. But you must dig a hole in the sand near where the boat is beached, and wait for him to start looking for you."

All that day the boy held the pipe for the skeleton. "And remember," said the skeleton, "don't return for a year. Then, if you will bring me a little tobacco, perhaps, it would be most beneficial. Indeed it would."

The boy hid in the sand until the man had disappeared among the trees, and then he ran to the boat and jumped in. As soon as they felt the movement, the swans flew back to the land, taking boat and boy with them safely among the deadly fish. And the boy went home, and stayed westwards for a year.

At the end of the year he made his way to the lake again. The swans were waiting. The island was unchanged.

"I've brought a new pipe, and pouches of tobacco," said the boy.

"You are more than considerate," said the skeleton. "The nesting season has been a great burden."

The boy lit the pipe, and the mice were soon cleared.

"Can I do anything more to help you?" said the boy. "You saved my life. Shall I bury you?"

"No," said the skeleton. "I would rather know the sun and the rain, the wind and the moon, and let them do their work. It is pleasanter here than in the dark."

So the boy built a hut on the lake shore, and each day he came with the swans to light the skeleton's pipe and to keep him company, until the sun and the rain, the wind and the moon had done their work, and nothing remained to tempt the busy mice.

The River God
(Of the River Mimram in Hertfordshire)

I may be smelly and I may be old,
Rough in my pebbles, reedy in my pools,
But where my fish float by I bless their swimming
And I like the people to bathe in me, especially women.
But I can drown the fools
Who bathe too close to the weir, contrary to rules.
And they take a long time drowning
As I throw them up now and then in a spirit of clowning.
Hi yih, yippity-yap, merrily I flow,
O I may be an old foul river but I have plenty of go.
Once there was a lady who was too bold
She bathed in me by the tall black cliff where the water
    runs cold,
So I brought her down here
To be my beautiful dear.
Oh will she stay with me will she stay
This beautiful lady, or will she go away?
She lies in my beautiful deep river bed with many a weed
To hold her, and many a waving reed.
Oh who would guess what a beautiful white face lies
    there
Waiting for me to smooth and wash away the fear

She looks at me with. Hi yih, do not let her
Go. There is no one on earth who does not forget her
Now. They say I am a foolish old smelly river
But they do not know of my wide original bed
Where the lady waits, with her golden sleepy head.
If she wishes to go I will not forgive her.

STEVIE SMITH

Wild Worms and Swooning Shadows

BRITAIN is a reasonably safe place for people to live in now, as far as animals are concerned. The last wolf was killed in 1743; the last wild boar in 1683; and the last dragon in 1614, or thereabouts.

In the British Museum there is a very old printed document that says:

"True and Wonderful!

A discourse relating a strange and Monstrous Serpent or Dragon, lately discovered, and yet living, to the great annoyance and divers slaughters both of men and cattle in Sussex, two miles from Horsham, in a wood called St. Leonard's Forest, and thirty miles from London, this present month of August, 1614.

To the Reader:

I believe, ere thou hast read this little all, thou wilt not doubt of one, but believe there are many serpents in England.

Farewell.

By A.R. (He that would send better news if he had it.)

In Sussex there is a pretty market towne called Horsham; near which is a forest, called St. Leonard's Forest. And there, in a vast and unfrequented place; heathie; vaultie; full of unwholesome shades, and overgrown hollows; this serpent is thought to be bred. Certaine and too true it is that there it yet lives. And it hath been seen within half a mile of Horsham; a wonder no doubt most terrible and noisome to the inhabitants thereabouts.

There is always in his tracke or path left a glutinous and slimie matter, which is very corrupt and offensive to the scent, which must needs be very dangerous; for though the corruption of it cannot strike the outward parts of a man, yet by receiving it into our breathing organs (the nose or mouth), it is mortall and deadlie.

The Serpent or Dragon, as some call it, is reputed to be nine feet, or rather more, in length, and shaped almost in the form of the axle-tree of a cart; a quantitie of Thickness in the middest, and somewhat smaller at both ends.

The scales along his backe seem to be blackish, and so much as is discovered under his bellie, appeareth to be red; for I speak of no nearer discription than a reasonable ocular distance; for coming too near it hath already been too dearlie pay'd for.

It is likewise discovered to have large feet, and rids away as fast as a man can run.

He is of countenance very proud, and at the sight or hearing of man or cattell, will raise his necke upright, and seem to listen and loke about with great arrogance.

There are like wise on either side of him discovered two great bunches, so big as a large foote ball, and as some think, will growe into wings. But God I hope will so defend the poore people of the neighbourhood, that he shall be destroyed before he growe so fledge."

I presume he was. Otherwise we should have heard more about it. And although, by the description, he must have been a typical dragon of folk-lore, he was a bit on the small side. And he was mild, compared with the one that lived near Rotherham.

"This dragon had two furious wings,
  Each one upon each shoulder;
With a sting in its tail, as long as a flayl,
  Which made him bolder and bolder.

He had long claws, and in his jaws
  Four-and-forty teeth of iron;
With a hide as tough as any buff,
  Which did him round environ."

So a fully grown "loathly worm", as dragons were called, was quite a problem. "Worm", in the Middle Ages, was used to mean generally any monstrous or destructive creature. Even a plague of locusts was once referred to as "a visitation of wyld wormes".

The stories of dragons in Britain are all variations on the well-known legend of a terrible worm that lays waste the land, and drains it of milk, cattle and girls until it is killed by a brave knight. There is not much to the legend, but what is intriguing is the area where it is found.

The north-east of England seems to have been thick with dragons at one time; and several ancient families are supposed to have earned their estates as a reward for disposing of a worm. For instance, there was one killed at Bishop Auckland by a knight called Pollard, who received from the bishop as much land as he could ride round while the bishop dined. This estate, called Pollard's Dene, was held by the family, not on payment of a rent or tax, but by the carrying out of a short ceremony.

When a new bishop entered the district for the first time, he was met by the senior member of the Pollard family, carrying an ancient sword, which was handed to the bishop with these words:

"My lord, I, in behalf of myself, as well as several others, possessors of the Pollard's lands, do humbly present your Lordship with this sword at your first coming here; where-with, as the tradition goeth, the knight Pollard slew of old a venemous serpent, which did much harm to man and beast; and by performing this service, we hold our lands."

The bishop took the sword, and then immediately gave it back, wishing the holder of Pollard's Dene health and a long enjoyment of the land. Customs of this sort lasted well into the Nineteenth Century in the north-east.

Now dragons are found in the legends of nearly every country in the world. They seem to be spirits of thunder and lightning, or the forces of darkness and winter that are always conquered by the sun. Belief in them is thousands of years old. But this tale of the girl-milk-and-cow-stealing serpent is strangely concentrated in the areas that suffered most from Viking raids. I wonder if our loathly, wild worms are perhaps also a memory of the Vikings' long, dragon-headed ships. Anyone who could strike a decisive blow against them would deserve a bishop's gratitude.

But worms are not the only strange beasts that live in these places. Here is an account of another creature.

"It was between eight and nine o'clock at night. Josh and I were in a lane near Geldeston, when we met Mrs. Smith, and she started to walk with us. And then I heard some-thing behind us, like the sound of a dog running. I thought it was some farmer's dog, and paid little attention to it; but it kept on at the back of us, pit-pat-pit-pat-pit-pat.

'I wonder what that dog wants,' I said to Mrs. Smith.

'What dog do you mean?' said she, looking all round.

'Why, can't you hear it?' said I. 'It's been following us for the last five minutes or more!'

I was walking between Josh and Mrs. Smith, and I lay

hold of Mrs. Smith's arm, and she says, 'I can hear it now; it's in front of us: look, there it be!'

And sure enough, just in front of us was what looked like a big black dog; but it wasn't a dog at all; it was the Hateful Thing, that had been seen hereabouts before.

It kept in front of us until it came to the churchyard, when it went right through the wall, and we saw it no more."

But what they had seen was a Dog of Darkness.

This animal has almost as many names as places where it appears. At Leiston, in Suffolk, it is called the Galleytrot, and haunts the churchyard and surrounding lanes. The connection with churches may be due to a custom found in the Middle Ages of burying a dog alive under the corner-stone of the church, so that its ghost could keep watch over the churchyard, and drive off witches.

At Cromer, the Dog is called Black Shuck. Elsewhere, it is the Swooning Shadow, the Snarleyow, the Skriker, and the Moddy Dhoo. In Yorkshire, Durham and Northumberland it is known as the Bargeist.

The villages around Leeds have a supernatural dog called Padfoot. "It is sometimes visible, sometimes invisible, but ever and anon padding lightly in the rear of people, then again before them, or at their side. In size it is somewhat larger than a sheep, with long, smooth hair. It is certainly safer to leave the creature alone."

A story is told of a man, whose way was being ob-structed by the Padfoot. He kicked the thing, and was immediately dragged along through hedge and ditch to his home and left under his own window.

Of all the creatures of folk-lore, belief in the Dog has survived most strongly to the present day. And, as with the wild worms, the legends are grouped most thickly in the areas of Viking penetration—all along the east coast, from Northumberland to Kent; the Isle of Man; and the coastal parishes of North Wales.

Odin, the chief god of the Vikings, had two hunting hounds, Geri and Freki. They went with him at all times.

That is true. But so is this:

"Should you never set eyes on our Norfolk Snarleyow, you may perhaps doubt his existence, and, like other learned folks, tell us that his story is nothing but the old myth of the black hounds of Odin, brought to us by the Vikings who long ago settled down on the Norfolk coast.

"Scoffers at Black Shuck there have been in plenty. But now and again one of them has come home late on a dark, stormy night, with terror written large on his face, and after that night he has scoffed no more."

And here is a transcript of a tape recording that I made recently. The words are exactly as they were spoken:

"Well this thing happened eight or nine years ago, when I was doing my National Service on a radar station in East Anglia.

I say 'in' East Anglia; actually we were right on the edge of it, surrounded by sea, river and marsh; just this one road connecting us with the mainland.

Well, the camp was divided into two main areas; the first place you came to was the actual work-site, and then beyond it, at the very end of the road, were the living quarters.

Now these centred round a large manor house, which had either been bought, or leased, or pinched or something from a very well-known Suffolk family, who'd lived there.

The main drive that went down from the manor house to the work-site had been laid out with particular care.

And I remember, there was one night in late spring or early summer that I was going down from the living quarters to do a late shift. It was a very still, clear night, and rather warm, I think.

Well now; this drive was lined by tall trees. And I remember there was a pretty full moon that night. I'd been doing fire-picket, or special duty, or something—I don't know. Anyway, it was about one o'clock in the morning, and I was all by myself.

Well, just before you get to the work-site, there's a couple of gates that lead out on to the public road. There's a big gate, for road traffic; and a smaller one at the side for pedestrians.

Anyway, I'd got, I suppose, just over a hundred yards away from the gates, when I heard the sound of the smaller one being shut. Nothing very unusual about that.

But as I got a bit nearer, it occurred to me that it must have been someone going up to the work-site, like I was, because there was no one coming towards me. Then I also began to hear what sounded like footsteps. It was odd, because, as I say, I couldn't see anyone, but at least it was still a fairly indistinct sound.

Well, by now I was only sixty or seventy yards away from this gate, and I could still hear this sound. And then, suddenly, I realized they weren't a human being's footsteps. They were an animal's. Something like a very big dog. Pit-pat, pit-pat, pit-pat-sort-of-thing. And they were coming towards me. And I couldn't see a sign of the thing.

And then suddenly, you know, crack! this cold fear suddenly hits you. You feel absolutely trapped.

I stood dead still. And this pit-pat, pit-pat, pit-pat comes right up to within inches of me; and goes on past me up the drive; and there's not a thing to be seen; not a thing.

It's an absolutely dead still night. You could hardly even hear any wind in the trees; and I was absolutely rooted to the spot.

And then, wham! I took off like a rocket.

I raced down the drive, through the gate and up to the work-site. I asked the policeman on duty, has anyone come down from here during the last half hour?

'No,' he says. 'You're the first that's been or come for three quarters of an hour.'"

That was a friend of mine. He might have been a scoffer —if he had known that there was anything to scoff at. But he has never heard of Black Shuck.

Loki

The Norse gods were more like neighbouring farmers than remote deities, and they were not immortal. At the end, even though they were on the right side, they lost.

Loki seems to have been left over from an earlier religion, and it shows in his nature. He was quick and subtle among gods who were strong and direct—in much the same way that an Irishman baffles the English. At first he was more mischievous than evil, and only later did he become black right through.

THE gods of Asgard could not live for ever—not even Odin, the father of all. They were gods who would grow bent, and weak, and die like ordinary men. But they owned a treasure that was more than the gold of the earth and the pearls of the sea. Her name was Idun, and she kept a box of magic apples.

These apples held the power of everlasting youth. Their taste was April, and they were the colour of the sun. But not only the gods loved Idun's beauty and wanted to taste the Apples of Life. Not only gods wanted to live for ever. . . .

One day Odin, Hoenir and Loki were travelling far from Asgard. The three gods were often together, for between them they had made the first man and woman out of two logs—an ash and an elm. So from time to time they left Asgard to visit these moving logs called men.

By the end of the day, the gods were tired and hungry, and they were in a desolate place without any house or shelter. Loki killed an ox, and built a fire to roast it on.

He blew the wood red and white, and the bark flared like beards.

Loki stood back. "That's the fire!" he said. "Sit yourself down, Odin Allfather; the ox will soon be done. Oh, look at those legs! And that shoulder! We'll not do so bad for supper tonight. Eh? Ah, that's the fire!"

"I'm cold," said Odin.

"Come a bit nearer, then, Allfather. These flames will put a glow on you. It takes Loki to build a real fire. Oh, the gravy of it! Oh, the crackling! The darling sweet marrow!"

Loki drooled and danced around the fire. Hoenir turned the ox.

"I am still cold," said Odin.

"Come nearer, then," said Loki.

"My feet are in the fire already."

Loki dropped on his forearms and blew the fire until he fell sideways in a coughing fit.

"The fire is big enough," said Odin. "The flames are cold."

"There's no point in roasting this ox," said Hoenir. "It's not even singed."

Loki turned to face the darkness that enclosed them. "There's something funny going on," he said. "Where is it?" His gaze travelled round; and up; and down; and up— there was a tall shape in the head of a pine tree beyond the fire, an eagle bigger than a man sat there and watched the three gods.

"Hey! You!" shouted Loki. "Have you been putting a spell on this fire?"

"I have," said the eagle.

"Then you can take it off again!"

The eagle did not move.

"Do you hear me? Take the spell off the fire! We're starving!"

"And if I do, what will you give me?" said the eagle.

"Give you? Give you? It's what I'll be giving you if you don't, you moth-eaten sparrow!"

"Quiet, Loki," said Odin. "Old eagle, old eagle, grey-crested tonight: what do you want? I am Odin."

"I know you all," said the eagle. "My share of the ox is what I am asking if I roast it for you."

"You shall have that. Come down."

The eagle dropped like a dark banner before the fire, and the flames joined sky and earth under the boom of its wings. The ox was roasted.

Loki glared sideways at the eagle, but he was the first to reach for the ox when the meat was done.

"Wait," said Odin. "The cook must choose his share."

"But, Allfather—"

"Wait. Now, eagle, take your share."

"I shall," said the eagle. "And here is your share."

From the beak and talons there dropped a few picked bones.

"My supper!" screamed Loki. "That's where manners gets you! My lovely ox!" He cast about him in the rage of his hunger, and tore a branch from the trunk of a tree, and brought it down with the force of his godhead upon the eagle's back. The eagle laughed. It was not the laugh of an eagle, but the laugh of a giant.

He leapt into the air, and the branch clung to his back, and Loki clung to the branch and could not let go. For an instant wings and feathers and the white limbs of Loki swirled upwards in the firelight, and then Hoenir and Odin were alone in that desolate place before a cold fire and silence.

For Loki in his roaring height there was soon no star-point of red to mark the ground, but there was the booming cloud above him, and the numb grip of his hands on the branch, stronger than he could grip.

"Put me down!" he cried. "Put me down, you mangy rooster! What do you think you are doing? Let me go!"

"Let you go, Loki? Shall I? Now?" said the eagle.

"Yes!—No! Nononononono! You wouldn't! No-o-o-o-o-o—!"

The eagle laughed like his wings. "Not yet, Loki. Higher! Higher!"

"Oh, my arms! Oh, I'm freezing!"

"Higher! Higher!"

"What do you want? What are you doing it for? I never harmed you."

"I am Thiassi the Storm Giant," said the eagle. "I am Thiassi—"

"—Oh dear oh—"

"—and I have caught a god!"

"Put me down again, there's a good lad," said Loki.

"Yes, Loki, yes! But higher! Higher!"

"What are you going to do?"

"I am going to take you so high," said Thiassi, "that the night will paint you black with frost; so high, that when I drop you you will never reach the earth."

"Never—reach—the—earth?"

"You will fall so far, so fast, that you will burn in the air like a shooting star, and never reach the ground."

"Now what do you want to go to all that trouble for?"

"It is no trouble," said Thiassi. "But if I set you free unhurt, what will you give as ransom?"

"Ransom," said Loki. "That's it. I could fix that. Yes. Anything. Just you say. You've come to the right one. Oh yes."

"You promise?"

"I promise, all right," said Loki. "Just you put me down nice and easy, and I'll do anything for you."

"Anything?"

"Oh yes. Anything. You'll see. But please: down: yes? My arms are out of their sockets—"

"Then bring me," said Thiassi, "Idun and the Apples of Life."

"What?" said Loki. "Idun? Oh no. I can't. Not Idun. Anything but Idun."

"Then higher, Loki! Higher!"

"Ay! Oo! Ah! Oh!"

"Higher! Higher! Higher!"

"Oh! Ah! Oo! Ay!"

"Higher!"

"All right! All right! Idun!"

"And the Apples."

"And the Apples!"

"Without fail."

"Without fail!"

"Good," said Thiassi. "Good. Then down we go."

Idun was walking by the fountains of Asgard. She was so beautiful that wherever she went flowers sprang in her footsteps.

"Hello, there!" said Loki.

"Hello, Loki. I thought you were away," said Idun.

"Yes. Well, you see, I got back sooner than expected. Are Odin and Hoenir in Asgard yet?"

"No," said Idun. "We thought they were with you."

"So they were. So they were. But I came home by a different route; and a tiring one it's been, I'll tell you. I'm not myself at all."

"You should have an apple, then," said Idun. She opened her golden casket. "Here, Loki. This will make you better."

"Do you think I could be having just a bite?"

"Of course. Here. Take it."

Loki held the apple in his hand. His teeth sank through the crisp and burnished gold. He chewed for a while, his eyes closed in concentration, then he lay back against a fountain stone, and smiled, and sighed his pleasure.

"Oh, that's good. Yes, it's a darling sweet apple. Mmmm. Yes. Nearly perfect. Delicious. Thanks, Idun. Bless you for a dear girl."

"What do you mean?" said Idun. "'Nearly perfect'?"

"Think nothing of it," said Loki. "A slip of the tongue, my dear. It's a grand apple."

"But my apples are the Apples of Life. They are perfect!"

"Well—this morning—I tasted—well, no, perhaps I'm wrong," said Loki. "Forget it."

Idun stamped her foot. "There are no apples like mine!"

"Yes, perhaps you're right," said Loki. "Don't take on. Perhaps you're right."

Idun hit him with the casket. "Tell me! You're hiding something from me!"

"Ouch! Well—er—ay—um—"

"Please!"

"Well, you see," said Loki, "I was coming back through the forest just now towards Asgard, all hot and bothered like, and there was this apple tree with golden apples on it. Don't fret yourself, Idun, my dear. It was probably because I was feeling so parched. You've some grand apples."

"You think those on the tree were better! Where is it? Show me! Take me there now!"

"Hey, it's not as bad as that. You don't want to be trailing out into the forest."

Idun began to cry.

"Ah, you'd charm the spots off a thrush," said Loki. "Come on, then. You'd best bring your apples with you to compare. It's quite a way we've to go—"

So Idun went with Loki, and he took her through a dark forest that endured from the morning to the setting of the sun. As the darkness grew, Idun stumbled and wept with exhaustion, yet she would not touch her apples, in case she ate the best. But at last they came to a clearing, and Loki made her sit on a tree trunk.

"You rest there, my dear, while I find the place. It's just by here somewhere in the thicket. I'll give you a shout when I've found it."

Idun nodded, too tired to speak.

She waited.

And waited.

"Loki?"

Waited.

"Loki?"

A wind grew in the forest, coming nearer.

"Loki! Lo–ki–i–i—"

"Idun! Iduu–u–u–uun!" droned the wind.

"Who's that? Who's there?"

"Idunnnnnn—"

Thiassi folded his wings around the clearing. "Idun. Come with me."

The wind and the screams died away, far to the North.

"Well, that's it," said Loki. "You can't say I don't keep my promise."

At first, no one noticed that Idun was missing from Asgard. But soon, one by one, the gods began to feel a stiffness, a heaviness, a weary weight of years. Brightness went from the eye, spring from the step. Winter was in their bones. Messengers rode through Asgard, and then through all the world: but Idun was not found.

Then Odin summoned Loki to a meeting of the gods.
"Where is Idun?"

"I wish I knew," said Loki. "I wish I knew."

"Where is Idun?"

"I'm telling you, Allfather. I wish I knew. She'll be somewhere, no doubt."

"Loki, I have asked, and no one has seen Idun since the day you returned to Asgard, the day you returned so quickly to Asgard after fighting the Storm Giant."

"Please," said Loki. "It was nothing. You'll embarrass me, Allfather. He didn't take much finishing off."

"So you told us. I think that you may be the cleverest of the gods, Loki: but that does not mean you are wise. Where is Idun?"

"How should I know?"

"I think that you do know," said Odin. "Loki, there is an ash tree that grows above this hall."

"Yes, Allfather. You made it yourself. It's the biggest thing in the world. Oh, it's a grand ash tree."

"Yggdrasil."

"Yes, that's its name, Allfather: a beautiful tree up there in the sky. It's a real credit to you."

"And its root is deep."

"It is. It is, to be sure. Well, it has to be, doesn't it?"

"It goes deep," said Odin. "It reaches far below the world, beyond the Strand of Corpses, far into the darkness. And there in the darkness lives the serpent Nidhug."

"Oh, that terrible monster! Don't mention him, Allfather. There's no luck in it."

"And the serpent gnaws at the root to kill the tree. And we know that when Yggdrasil falls, the gods will die."

Loki saw that the doors of the hall were now guarded. "Shall we talk about something more cheerful, Allfather?"

"And the gods will die unless Idun returns. We shall grow old, and Yggdrasil will fall. We must do all we can to save ourselves, Loki."

"They're bad times we're in; yes."

"Loki, if you do not tell us what has happened to Idun, you will be bound with iron chains to the root of Yggdrasil, far from the light. Nidhug will eat you first. And that way we shall win a little time."

"You wouldn't do that, Allfather—"

"Where is Idun?"

"Now wait a minute, Allfather—"

"Take him," said Odin to the gods.

"Allfather—!"

"Bind him."

"Allf—!"

"Idun, Loki. Nidhug is waiting."

"All right, all right!" wept Loki in anger. "But it's your fault, too! You should have rescued me. You'd never have had that ox in the first place if it hadn't been for me. 'Higher and higher!' he kept shouting. 'Higher and higher!' He was going to drop me so as I'd burn up. 'Higher!' he kept shouting. 'Higher!—Higher!' What else could I do? If I hadn't promised to get Idun for him he'd have dropped me!"

"It was not an easy choice," said Odin. "I can see that. So you will be given one chance to make things right. You will go to the Storm Giant's castle. Go in the shape of a falcon. Bring back Idun and the Apples of Life."

Then Loki flew far and long over the Back of the Sea until he came to the Storm Giant's castle. He found Idun sitting in a high tower. He landed on the window ledge.

"Hey! Idun!"

"Hello, Falcon. How did you know my name?" she said. "It's me!"

"Loki!"

"Not so loud. Where's that Thiassi?"

"He's not here," said Idun. "He won't be back for a long time. Have you come to rescue me?"

"I have that. Are you all right? Where are the apples?"

"They are all safe. Thiassi is very kind to me, even though I can't let him have the god's apples. He's very sad and lonely. He's not really cruel."

"I've not found him over fond," said Loki. "Come up now: let's be off."

"But how?" said Idun. "I can't fly, and—oh! What's happened? I feel all small and round!"

"You're a hazel nut, my dear," said Loki. "That's to carry you light and easy. I've no doubt that meek little Thiassi of yours will be after us before we reach Asgard, so here's some magic to help us on our way."

Loki grabbed Idun in his claws, and flew fast. But when he came within sight of Asgard he heard the wings of Thiassi behind him. But Odin had guessed at the pursuit, and the gods had piled brushwood on the walls of Asgard, and the moment Loki crossed the ramparts the bonfires were lit, and the flames shot upwards. Thiassi could not stop in time, and was caught in the fire. He fell dead in Asgard at Odin's feet.

Idun stood by and wept.

"Now what's the matter?" said Loki. "He nearly had us. You're safe now. There'll be no more trouble from him."

"He was so kind, and so lonely," said Idun. "He was splendid in the sky, and now he is charred plumes."

"I am sorry for his death," said Odin. "He should not

have died. No one can be blamed for wanting to eat of the Apples of Life."

"Don't let him lie there," said Idun. "Put him back in the sky."

"I can't give him life again," said Odin. "But I'll do what I can."

And Odin took the Storm Giant's eyes, and set them as two stars in the sky, so that Thiassi would not lie in the earth, but would soar for ever and look down upon the backs of eagles. For the gods held it no wrong to cherish Idun and the Apples of Life.

Baldur the Bright

TO Frigga the wife of Odin were born twin sons. One was Hodur: he was dark and silent, and blind as winter. The other was Baldur. He was fair and full of song. His brow was like the day, and he knew the magic of trees and the virtues of summer flowers, He lived in Asgard in a hall of golden pillars thatched with silver. He knew the secret of buds. He knew the dance of the bees. He knew the heart of the rose. He knew all things but one. He did not know his own fate.

There had never been such light and laughter in Asgard before Baldur came; and the gods loved him—all except Loki, whose fame and wit were now like the flames of a fire that are paled by the sun.

Loki kept watch in Asgard: waiting.

"What's the matter with Baldur?" said Odin one day. Loki heard, and came close, unseen. "He looks ill," said Odin.

"He has had the same bad dream for nights on end," said Frigga. "But he can never remember what it is. He wakes up exhausted and sweating and afraid. I think it's a warning of some harm that will be done to him."

"Harm!" said Odin. "Wife, we have a son who is the gold of Asgard! No one will hurt him! The streams are bright for his passing by, the skies blue. Only his hair is yellower than the corn that grows in our fields since he came to us."

"But he is pale and ill," said Frigga. "I think he may die."

"He won't. I forbid it."

"Allfather, you are strong, but you can't change fate."

"He will not die. He shall not die," said Odin. "It's only a dream—"

"So are the Shadowlands," said Frigga. "Yet they are more real than life."

"Then I shall ride to the Shadowlands!" said Odin. "They will tell me there, since they know the deaths of all."

"But it's so far to the Land of the Dead. A lot could happen while you were gone. Start at once," said Frigga. "And I'll do what I can. Baldur must be kept safe."

Odin left Asgard and rode for the Shadowlands. And Frigga sent Hermod, the messenger of the gods, to the North, to the South, to the East, to the West, to the whole world, to ask all things to promise that they would not harm Baldur. And this promise was given.

Every living creature that walked or swam or flew or crept or slept, and every plant that grew, and the cold rocks, and the sea, and the winds of the air—all creation gave this promise, to keep Baldur safe from harm, for their love of him.

This was the promise that Hermod took back to Asgard, and Frigga's heart was at rest.

But Loki put on the clothes of an old woman, and made his way disguised to Odin's hall. Frigga was sitting by the door.

"Good day to you, my Lady."

"Good day, old woman. Who are you? Are you a stranger to Asgard?"

"My name is—Thok," said Loki. "Indeed, indeed, I have come to hear the wonderful news. Is it true what they are saying now, my Lady—that all creation has promised not to hurt your fine upstanding son?"

"It is," said Frigga. "Baldur is loved by all."

"Ah, what it is to have a son a mother can be proud of! And is it true what they are saying—not only bird and beast and fish, but even lifeless things?"

"They will not hurt my son."

"Well, well, there's a wonder. It's lucky you are, my Lady, and a proud day for sure."

"It is, Thok, it is."

"And is it really true? Forgive me, my Lady, but poor old Thok's brains can't be doing with such a wonder all at once. My, what it is to be a mother! The whole world won't hurt him. Eh—! The whole world. Not—even the —the smallest thing—not a grain of sand, not—"

"Well—there was just one—"

"Oh, my Lady—!"

"Well, there was one tiny shoot of mistletoe Hermod didn't ask," said Frigga. "It was too young to promise: such a weak thing. It's probably dead already. It was growing by the doorpost of the Warriors' hall, right where they charge in and out. Those men get drunk every night. It will have been flattened by now."

"That's a blessing, then, my Lady. Ah, Baldur's the lucky young man."

Loki went straight to the Warriors' hall, and found the tiny mistletoe shoot among the rubbish by the door. And he took it, and reared it. He nursed it on black things without a name, on gravemound earth, and sang evil runes above. And the mistletoe grew straight as death and hard as frost, and when it was the size, Loki cut it, and from its wood made an arrow.

Odin returned to Asgard. His face was hidden below

his dark hood, but he moved as if he carried bad news.

Frigga ran out to greet him. Her face was flushed, and she did not notice Odin's slow tread.

"Come in, come in! I've so much to tell you!"

"I have been to the Shadowlands," said Odin.

"Well, sit down and listen," said Frigga. "While you've been galloping about I've been doing something useful. Everything is all right now!"

"How do you know?" said Odin. His voice was stretched over grief. "And what is that laughter? There should be no laughter!"

"That's my surprise for you!" said Frigga.

"There should be no laughter!"

"Come and look out of the window. It's the latest game. See. Baldur stands under that oak, and all the gods throw things at him. It's all right. Look, he's not hurt. It doesn't matter what they throw—spears, axes, stones, knives. They all bounce off without hurting him. Isn't he kind and patient to stand there so that the others can have their fun?"

"What does this mean?" said Odin.

"It takes a mother to look after her son. While you were riding up and down I made all creation promise not to hurt Baldur. See! Nothing touches him! He's safe now. He can't be killed."

"Frigga. Frigga. There are tables laid in the Shadowlands, and couches, and gold rings. I have seen dark velvet spread, and the meadhorn filled with sleep for Baldur. They have made a banquet in the Shadowlands for our son. Let the gods play: it will soon be night."

Among the leaves of green holly Hodur stood apart from the merriment. The branches rustled, and a voice spoke in his ear.

"Now what's all this? Hodur, is it you looking so sad and left out of the sport? You should be enjoying yourself with all the others. It's a great thing to know we'll be having Baldur with us always. Aren't you celebrating?"

"It's Loki, isn't it?" said Hodur. "Oh, don't worry about me."

"Is it perhaps you're feeling a wee bit jealous of brother Baldur the Bright?"

"No!" said Hodur. "I can't help wishing I wasn't blind, that's all. They're having such a good game over there, and I can't share it."

"You're wishing you could see to throw something at Baldur, eh?" said Loki.

"Yes," said Hodur. "They say it's marvellous to watch. Things stop in mid air, or turn corners, or slow down, and he doesn't feel any of it, because all creation has promised not to hurt him. Even Thor's hammer was gentle."

"Was it now? Ah, it's a wonderful thing, indeed. But look, there's no reason for you to be missing out. There is not."

"But I can't see!"

"I'll help you," said Loki. "Now here's my bow. There. You've got it. It's a good firm bow. That's it. Oh, you're bending it fine. Try again—that's it!"

"Yes: I can do that. Yes: it's all right."

"Of course it is. You're a natural. Now then. Here's my very best arrow. Feel how long and straight she is: she's made of very special wood. Oh, she flies like a bird. She goes where you put her. There's the notch: now the string: and her point:—so. Have you got her? Now try her, but don't shoot. Easy: pull back, smooth and gentle—that's my boy. Oh, you're the champion! Let her go slowly, slowly—and lower. There."

"Yes! Loki, I can do it!"

"Of course you can! Now I'll turn you in the right direction and aim for you."

"Baldur will be pleased. He's always trying to make me do things like the others."

"Good. Good," said Loki. "Now then. There. Like that: yessss—. A shade to your left. Now—draw—right—back, till you feel the string on your nose. That's it. Lift the point a bit. A bit more. Now—hold—steady—and—fire!"

In the cold silence after the scream Hodur swung his head, trying to grasp sounds. "What? What was that? What's happened?" he said.

Loki's voice answered him but now distant in space and heart. "I'm afraid, my dear, it looks like you've killed your brother."

The gods took Baldur and laid him in Ringhorn, his own dragon-ship. They built his funeral pyre about him and brought garlands of flowers, and jewels, and precious work. They put his winged helmet on his head, and his sword between his hands. And then they set fire to the sweet pine branch, and they sent Ringhorn westward over the sea, and stood watching until the last flame of its burning faded from the sky. Then their hearts broke: and on the stark shore it was night.

"Baldur!—Come back!"

"Frigga," said Odin. "Our son is dead."

She stood in the foam of the water's edge. "I won't let him be dead! I won't—let him! I—won't!"

"We can't change fate," said Odin.

"I can!—Hermod! Hermod, you are quick, you are brave, you are strong. Hermod, ride to the Shadowlands now: bring him back: bring my son: bring Baldur."

"But, my Lady," said Hermod, "it is grief—"

"Go to the queen of the Shadowlands. Ask her. Ask Hela to give me back my son."

"My Lady! Hela does not give up her prey. Baldur's dead, my Lady."

"Is Odin's wife to bow to Hela? Bring back my son!"

So Hermod rode for Hela's land. He rode down Asabru, the coloured bridge of fire and water and air that spans the sky, down to the Shadowlands of the North. Nine days and nights he rode without stopping before he crossed the boundary—a bridge of crystal arched with gold, hung on a single hair.

He rode through a wood with trees and leaves of iron, through the dark and the cold and the mist, over a river of naked swords, till he came to the hall of the queen of the Shadowlands. The name of her hall was Misery.

But Hermod was not afraid to give his message, and all night long he pleaded with Hela to let Baldur go free to Asgard.

"So Frigga weeps," said Hela. "And if I listened to every mother's prayer?"

"It is not just Frigga who wants her son," said Hermod. "We all want Baldur to come back. The whole world grieves for him. All mothers weep."

"My music is their tears," said Hela.

"Then let me bring you music—and set Baldur free."

"What do you mean? Yes? Yes! That would be joy! The whole world in tears. All creation sing for me. Yes! You shall have Baldur, then, if all things weep for him. Yes! But if one, one does not, I keep him fast."

Then back rode Hermod from Hela's hall, and then through all the world: to the North, to the South, to the East, to the West, to ask all things to weep for Baldur. And this was given. Every living creature that walked or swam or flew or crept or slept, and every plant that grew, and the cold rocks, and the sea, and the winds of the air—all creation wept for Baldur dead.

Hermod rode for Asgard through their tears. But when he was close to Asgard's walls he passed a cave mouth. Deep in the cave he saw something move, something black, with dull red eyes like coal. And the cave was silent.

"Who's there?" he said.

"An old woman," said a voice.

"Then weep. All things weep for Baldur."

"I don't. He's dead."

"He will come back to Asgard if all creation drops tears for him."

"He'll not come back for me."

"But he'll bring light and joy and meadow laughter!"

"I don't know them. I don't need him."

"What are you if you will not weep?" said Hermod.

The voice answered him, slow and chanting:

"I   Am   Thok

"I   Weep   Dry   Tears

"He   Gave   Me   No   Gladness

"Let   Hela   Keep   Her   Prey."

And so, through the malice of Loki, the tears of the world were lost, and Baldur was seen in Asgard no more. From this time the glory of Asgard began to fade. Blind Hodur was killed in vengeance, and Loki was caught and chained deep under the earth. But the gods could not be saved. Baldur was gone, and blood had been shed: murder grew from murder, and grief from grief, and from these came war: a sword age: a wolf age: winter: and the world's end.

The Beast

Something that was not there before
has come through the mirror
into my room.

It is not such a simple creature
as at first I thought—
from somewhere it has brought a mischief

that troubles both silence and objects
and now left alone here
I weave intricate reasons for its arrival.

They disintegrate. Today in January, with
the light frozen on my window, I hear outside
a million panicking birds, and know even out there

comfort is done with; it has shattered
even the stars, this creature
at last come home to me.

BRIAN PATTEN

Glooskap

GLOOSKAP and his brother Malsum the Wolf made the world. Their mother died at their birth, and from her they took the things of their choice. Glooskap shaped the sun and the moon, animals, fish and men, and Malsum gave mountains, ravines, snakes and all that he hoped would be a plague. He was so wrong that Glooskap killed him, and then went on with the work.

Glooskap subdued the sorcerer Win-pe, and Pamola of the Night, and the Kewawkque giants, and the Medecolin wizards, and the tribes of the witches and the goblins and the living dead. He levelled the hills, controlled the floods, and gave life to the maize.

"Ho," said Glooskap, "there is nothing I cannot command. The heavens turn for me."

But a woman of the Mohican laughed, and said, "There is in my tent, O Glooskap, one you have not conquered, nor shall you, for no power can overcome him."

"What is this god or wizard?" said Glooskap.

"His name is Wasis," she said. "And I advise you not to try him."

"Show me this Wasis," said Glooskap. "Is he greater than the Medecolin? I had strength of mind in plenty for them. Is he more terrible than the Kewawkque? They woke no fear in me. Is he more dangerous than Pamola of the Night? I carry no scars from that battle. Is he Huron or Tuscarora? Is he Cayuga or Mohawk? Oneida? Onondaga?

Is he Susquehannock? Is he Cherokee? Let him be all, and I shall conquer him!"

"He is none of these," said the woman, "and he sits on the floor of my tent."

Wasis sucked a piece of maple sugar, and crooned a little to himself. Glooskap stood in front of him, filling the tent with power.

"My visit is peace," said Glooskap. "Come you to me."

Wasis smiled at him, and did not move.

"I am not wrathful," said Glooskap. "Come to me." And he sang the song of the blackbird. Wasis sucked the maple sugar.

"The world obeys me!" shouted Glooskap. "Come!"

Wasis frowned.

"I fear no threat! Come to me on your knees!" roared Glooskap.

But Wasis did not.

Then Glooskap unleashed his rage, and the winds answered his cry about the tent, but Wasis opened his mouth and gave a scream that pierced the wind as an arrow through a bird in flight.

Glooskap brought all magic to his mind, and chanted spells, and summoned ghosts, and made the knots that raise the dead.

But Wasis closed his eyes, and slept.

Glooskap rushed from the tent and flung himself into the river, and the heat of his fury boiled the river dry.

"Goo," said Wasis.

And even now babies say this word, each remembering the day he conquered Glooskap, there by the tent floor, with maple sugar on his mouth.

A Game

They are throwing the ball
To and fro between them,
In and out of the picture.
She is in the painting
Hung on the wall
In a narrow gold frame.
He stands on the floor
Catching and tossing
At the right distance.
She wears a white dress,
Black boots and stockings,
And a flowered straw hat.
She moves in silence
But it seems from her face
That she must be laughing.
Behind her is sunlight
And a tree-filled garden;
You might think to hear
Birds or running water,
But no, there is nothing.
Once or twice he has spoken
But does so no more,
For she cannot answer.
So he stands smiling,
Playing her game
(She is almost a child),

Not daring to go,
Intent on the ball.
And she is the same.
For what would result
Neither wishes to know
If it should fall.

FLEUR ADCOCK

The Green Mist

SO you've heard tell of the boggarts, and all the horrid things of old times? You've heard of the voices of dead folks, and hands without arms, that came in the darklins, moaning and crying and beckoning all night through; todloweries dancing on the tussocks, and witches riding on the great black snags, that turned to snakes, and raced about with them in the water?

Ay, they were mischancy, unpleasant sort of bodies to do with, and I'm main glad as they were all gone before my days.

Well, in those times folk must have been unlike to now. Instead of doing their work in the week, and smoking their pipes on Sundays, in peace and comfort, they were always bothering their heads about something or other— or the church was doing it for them. The priests were always at them about their souls; and, what with hell and the boggarts, their minds were never easy.

The bogles were once thought a deal more on, and at darklins every night the folk would bear lights in their hands round their houses, saying words to keep them off; and would smear blood on the door sill to scare away the horrors; and would put bread and salt on the flat stones set up by the lane-side to get a good harvest; and would spill water in the four corners of the fields, when they wanted rain; and they thought a deal on the sun, for they reckoned as it made the earth, and brought the good and ill chances and I don't know what all. I reckon they made nigh everything as they saw and heard into great bogles; and they were always giving them things, or saying sort of prayers like, to keep them from doing the folk any evil.

Well, that was a long time ago. So there were, so to say, two churches; the one with priests and candles, and all that; the other just a lot of old ways, kept up all unbeknown and hidden-like, mid the folk themselves; and they thought a deal more on the old spells than on the service in the church itself. But as time went on the two got sort of mixed up, and some of the folks couldn't have told you if it were for one or the other as they done the things.

To Yule, in the churches, there were grand services, with candles and flags and what not; and in the cottages there were candles and cakes and grand doings; but the priests never knowed as many of the folks were only waking the dying year, and that the wine teemed upon the door sill to first cock-crow were to bring good luck in the new year. And I reckon as some of the folks themselves would do the old heathen ways and sing hymns meantime, with never a thought of the strangeness of it.

Still, there were many as kept to the old ways altogether, though they did it hidden like; and I'm going to tell you of one family as my grandfather knowed fine, and how they waked the Spring one year.

As I said before, I can't, even if I would, tell you all the things as they used to do; but there was one time of the year as they particularly went in for their spells and prayers, and that were the early Spring. They thought as the earth was sleeping all the winter; and that the bogles—call them what you will—had nobbut to do but mischief, for they'd nowt to see to in the fields: so they were feared on the long dark winter days and nights, in the middle of all sorts of unseen fearsome things, ready and waiting for a chance to play them evil tricks.

But as the winter went by, they thought as it were time to wake the earth from its sleeping and set the bogles to work, caring for the growing things, and bringing the harvest.

After that the earth were tired, and were sinking to sleep again; and they used to sing hushieby songs in the fields of the Autumn evens.

But in the Spring they went—the folk did as believed in the old ways—to every field in turn, and lifted a spud of earth from the mools; and they said strange and queer words, as they couldn't scarce understand themselves, but the same as had been said for hundreds of years. And every morning at the first dawn, they stood on the door sill, with salt and bread in their hands, watching and waiting for the green mist as rose from the fields and told that the earth were awake again; and the life were coming to the trees and the plants, and the seeds were bursting with the beginning of the Spring.

Well, there was one family as had done all that, year after year, for as long as they knowed of, just as their grandfathers had done it before them; and one winter they were making ready for waking the Spring.

They had had a lot of trouble through the winter, sickness and what not had been bad in the place; and the daughter, a ramping young maid, was growed white and waffling like a bag of bones, instead of being the prettiest lass in the village, as she had been before.

Day after day she grew whiter and sillier, till she couldn't stand upon her feet more than a new born babby, and she could only lay at the window, watching and watching the winter creep away.

And, "Oh, mother," she'd keep saying over and over again, "if I could only wake the Spring with you again, may be the green mist would make me strong and well, like the trees and the flowers and the corn in the fields."

And the mother would comfort her like, and promise that she'd come with them again to the waking, and grow as strong and straight as ever. But day after day she got whiter and wanner, till she looked like a snowflake fading in the sun; and day after day the winter crept by, and the waking of the Spring was almost there.

The poor maid watched and waited for the time for going to the fields, she had got so weak and sick that she knew she couldn't get there with the rest. But she wouldn't give up, for all that; and her mother must swear that she would lift the lass to the door sill, at the coming of the green mist, so as she might toss out the bread and salt on the earth her own self and with her own poor thin hands.

And still the days went by, and the folk were going on early morns to lift the spud in the fields; and the coming of the green mist was looked for every dawning.

And one even, the lass, as had been laying with her eyes fixed on the little garden, said to her mother, "If the green mist doesn't come in the morn's dawning, I'll not can wait for it longer. The mools is calling me, and the seeds are bursting as will bloom over my head. I know it well, mother. And yet, if I could only see the Spring wake once again—mother—I swear as I'd ask no more than to live as long as one of those cowslips as come every year by the gate, and to die with the first of them when the Summer is in."

The mother whisht the maid in fear; for the bogles and things as they believed in were always gainhand, and could hear owt as was said. They were never safe, never alone, the poor folk to then, with the things as they couldn't see, and couldn't hear, all round them.

But the dawn of the next day brought the green mist. It came from the mools, and happed itself round everything, green as the grass in Summer sunshine, and sweet-smelling as the herbs of the Spring. And the lass was carried to the door sill, where she crumbled the bread and salt on to the earth with her own hands, and said the strange old words of welcoming to the new Spring.

And she looked to the gate, where the cowslips grew, and then she was taken back to her bed by the window, when she slept like a babby, and dreamt of Summer and flowers and happiness.

Whether it was the green mist as done it, I can't tell you, but from that day she grew stronger and prettier than ever, and by the time the cowslips were budding she was running about and laughing like a very sunbeam in the old cottage. But she was always so white and wan, while she looked like a will-o-the-wyke flitting about; and on the cold days she'd sit shaking over the fire and look nigh dead, but when the sun came out, she'd dance and sing in the light, and stretch out her arms to it, as if she only lived by the warmness of it.

And by and by the cowslips burst their buds, and came in flower, and the maid was grown so strange and beautiful that they were nigh feared on her—and every morning she would kneel by the cowslips and water and tend them and dance to them in the sunshine, while the mother would stand begging her to leave them, and cried that she would have them pulled up by the roots and throwed away. But the lass only looked strange at her, and said—soft and low like:

"If you aren't tired of me, mother—never pick one of

them flowers; they'll fade of their selves soon enough; ay, soon enough, you know."

And the mother would go back to the cottage and greet over the work. But she never said nowt of her trouble to the neighbours—not till afterwards.

But one day a lad of the village stopped at the gate to chat with them, and by and by, whiles he was gossiping, he picked a cowslip and played with it. The lass didn't see what he had done; but as he said goodbye he gave it to her, smiling like, and thinking what a pretty maid she was.

She looked at the flower and at the lad, and all round about her; at the green trees, and the sprouting grass, and the yellow blossoms; and up at the golden shining sun itself; and all to once, shrinking as if the light she had loved so much were burning her, she ran into the house, without a spoken word, only a sort of cry, like a dumb beast in pain, and the cowslip catched close against her breast.

And then she never spoke again; but lay on the bed, staring at the flower in her hand and fading as it faded all through the day. And at the dawning there was only lying on the bed a wrinkled, white, shrunken dead thing, with in its hand a shrivelled cowslip. And the mother covered it over with the clothes, and thought of the beautiful joyful maid dancing like a bird in the sunshine by the golden nodding blossoms, only the day gone by.

The bogles had heard her and given her the wish. She had bloomed with the cowslips, and had faded with the first of them. It's as true as death.

Notes and Sources

AT the age of eight I discovered among my great-grandfather's books twelve volumes of Myths and Legends, published by Harrap between 1915 and 1917. It was an overwhelming experience. The books themselves were not children's books, and when I went back to them after a quarter of a century, I was stifled by the pedantry and lack of feeling for language shown by most of the editors, yet somehow the collective force of the material still came through.

Several of the stories in this present book originated for me in the Harrap volumes, although wherever possible I have traced each to its source and used that. The intention has been to convey the spirit rather than the letter, and where a text has appeared to be inferior to its contents I have changed it. For this reason it seems advisable to give an indication of the degree of meddling involved, and so I have adopted the following terminology:

Adapted: The least possible interference with the text: alterations usually limited to small excisions, or the addition of a gloss, to make the original clear to the general reader.

Freely adapted: A retelling from an outmoded text: may vary from the original in details of plot: often includes episodes from parallel motifs.

Transposed: An intensification of the above: the creation of what is almost a new story, based on a good idea in a poor setting.

There is a chain of command in inspiration, a passing on of excitement, anger or delight. If someone, some day, finds this book at the back of a cupboard in his great-grandfather's house, and feels as keenly what I, and the writers before me, have felt, we shall have served our purpose.

SOURCES

Prayer: Law Tricks, Act V: The Works of John Day: ed. A. H. Bullen: London 1881: vol. 2.

Introduction: The list of goblins is from The Discoverie of Witchcraft: Reginald Scot: London 1584: book viii.

Gobbleknoll: Transposed from the Sioux folktale of The Rabbit and Pahe-Wathahuni: Myths and Legends of the North American Indians: Lewis Spence: Harrap: 1916. Among the Sioux, The Rabbit was the personification of cunning.

John Connu Rider: Andrew Salkey says: "John Connu probably derived from a carnival spectacle in French West Africa during Slavery. 'John the Unknown' (the Connu being a contraction of the French word for 'unknown') was a figure that appeared in a celebration march across the planter's lawn on Sundays and high holidays for the slaves on the instigation of the planter's lady. John Connu would be joined by Horse Head, Patoo, the Owl, and other carnival dressed-up characters, and they would wheel and dance and cavort until they dropped from exhaustion. Today, the Jamaican Government keeps the whole thing going at Christmas. I like John Connu, and think he's of us; so I've written a little piece about him for the kids in the West Indies and for anybody else who wants to read it."

Vukub-Cakix: Freely adapted from an incident in Popol Vuh ("Collection of Leaves"), the Maya-Kiche mythology. v. The Popol Vuh: Lewis Spence: London 1908.

Tops or Bottoms: Transposed from Dialect and Folk Lore of Northampton-shire: T. Sternberg: London 1851. Little of the feel of dialect survives in Sternberg's text, apart from the sublime "When do we wiffle-waffle, mate?", so I have transposed the story into the rhythm and idiom of my own area, East Cheshire.

The Voyage of Maelduin: Adapted from the translation of Whitley Stokes: Revue Celtique: vol. ix and x: Paris 1889.

The Fort of Rathangan: Translated by Kuno Meyer: Ancient Irish Poetry: Constable: 1911.

Willow: Adapted from Ancient Tales and Folklore of Japan: R. Gordon Smith. A. and C. Black, 1908.

The Term: The Collected Earlier Poems: William Carlos Williams: MacGibbon and Kee: 1951.

Edward Frank and the Friendly Cow: Adapted from Relation of Apparitions of Spirits in the County of Monmouth and the Principality of Wales: Edward Jones: Newport: 1813. The Reverend Edward Jones appears to have been a gullible man, and he preserved some queer gossip.

Yallery Brown: Adapted from Legends of the Lincolnshire Carrs: M. C.

Balfour: Folk-Lore II: 1891. In this tale, and in *The Green Mist*, I have tried to avoid the obscurities of dialect without losing the vivid language.

Moowis: Freely adapted from the Algonquin legend: Spence: North American Indians: op. cit.

The Snowman: Collected Poems of Wallace Stevens: Alfred A. Knopf, Inc.: 1951.

The Lady of the Wood: Adapted from the Iolo MS: British Goblins: Wirt Sikes: Sampson Low, Marston, Searle and Rivington: London 1880.

A Voice Speaks from the Well: Penguin Book of English Verse: 1956.

Bash Tchelik: Freely adapted from the version of Woislav Petrovitch: Hero Tales and Legends of the Serbians: Harrap: 1917.

The Dark Guest: Ernest George Moll: Penguin Book of Australian Verse, ed. John Thompson, Kenneth Slessor and R. G. Howarth: 1958.

The Goblin Spider: Freely adapted from the version of F. Hadland Davis: Myths and Legends of Japan: Harrap: 1917.

The Tengu: Davis: op. cit.

The Secret Commonwealth: The opening paragraph is from Miscellanies upon Various Subjects: John Aubrey: MS 1696: published London 1890.

The quotations from Robert Kirk are from The Secret Commonwealth of Elves, Fauns and Fairies: Robert Kirk: MS 1691: published Longman and Co.: 1815.

The disappearance of Mr. Kirk is based on two sources:

(1) Sketches Descriptive of Picturesque Scenery in the Southern Confines of Perthshire: P. Grahame: Edinburgh 1806.

(2) Letters on Demonology and Witchcraft: Sir Walter Scott: London 1884.

The stories of John Jenkinson and of Iolo ap Hugh are adapted from Sikes: op. cit.

The Piper of Shacklow: A Yorkshire traditional verse from Household Tales with other Traditional Remains: S. O. Addy: David Nutt: 1895.

The Adventures of Nera: Adapted from the translation of Kuno Meyer: Revue Celtique: vol x: Paris 1889.

A Letter: Jones: op. cit.

Halloween: Anon. Faber Book of Children's Verse: 1953.

Great Head and the Ten Brothers: Freely adapted from the Iroquois legend: Spence: North American Indians: op. cit.

The Trade That No One Knows: Freely adapted from Petrovitch: op. cit.

Charm Against Witches: Traditional English verse: in A Treasury of Witchcraft: H. E. Wedeck: Vision Press: 1961, and Citadel Press, Inc., New York.

Tarn Wethelan: Freely adapted from Percy's Reliques of Ancient English Poetry: vol ii: Everyman No. 149: Dent: 1906, and Dover Publications, Inc., New York.

All in Green went My Love Riding: Poems 1923–1954: e. e. cummings: Harcourt, Brace & World, Inc.

Hoichi the Earless: Freely adapted from The Story of Mimi-Nashi-Hoichi; Kwaidan: Stories and studies of strange things: Lafcadio Hearn: Kegan Paul, Trench, Trubner and Co. Ltd.: 1904.

Meeting in the Road: 170 Chinese Poems: translated by Arthur Waley: Constable: 1939.

Ramayana: Adapted and condensed from the translation of Ananda K. Coomaraswamy: Myths of the Hindus and Buddhists: Harrap: 1918.

In the Strange Isle: Michael Roberts: Collected Poems: Faber: 1958.

The Smoker: Freely adapted from an Iroquois legend: Spence: North American Indians: op. cit.

The River God (Of the River Mimram in Hertfordshire): Stevie Smith: Selected Poems: Longmans, Green and Co.: 1962.

Wild Worms and Swooning Shadows: The Dragon of St. Leonard's Forest is in Harleian Miscellany No. 3: British Museum: 1809.

The verse of the Rotherham Dragon is in Notes on the Folk Lore of the Northern Counties of England and the Borders: W. Henderson: Longmans, Green & Co.: 1886.

Pollard's Dene: Henderson: op. cit.

The story of The Hateful Thing is in In the Footsteps of Borrow and Fitzgerald: Morley Adams: Jarrold and Co.: 1914.

Padfoot: Henderson: op. cit.

Snarleyow and Black Shuck: Highways and Byways in East Anglia: W. A. Dutt: n.d.

Loki: Freely adapted from the Prose Edda of Snorri Sturluson: translated by Brodeur: Oxford University Press: 1916.

Baldur the Bright: Freely adapted from Brodeur: op. cit.

The Beast: The Mersey Sound: Penguin Modern Poets: 1968.

Glooskap: Freely adapted from an Algonquin legend: Spence: North American Indians: op. cit.

A Game: Fleur Adcock: The Listener, 20 October 1966, p. 589: the British Broadcasting Corporation.

The Green Mist: Balfour: op. cit.

Acknowledgements

The Editor and Publishers are indebted to the following for permission to include copyright material in this book: The author, Andrew Salkey, for permission to include his poem *John Connu Rider*, © Andrew Salkey, 1969; MacGibbon and Kee, London, and New Directions Publishing Corporation, New York, for permission to include *The Term* by William Carlos Williams from COLLECTED EARLIER POEMS, © 1938, 1951 by William Carlos Williams; Faber and Faber Ltd., London, and Alfred A. Knopf, Inc., New York, for permission to include *The Snowman* by Wallace Stevens from COLLECTED POEMS; the author, Ernest Moll, for permission to include his poem *The Dark Guest*; MacGibbon and Kee, London, and Harcourt, Brace and World, Inc., New York, for permission to include *All in Green went My Love Riding*, copyright 1923, 1951, by e. e. cummings. Reprinted from his volume POEMS 1923–1954; Constable and Company Ltd., London, and Alfred A. Knopf, Inc., New York, for permission to include *Meeting in the Road* from 170 CHINESE POEMS adapted by Arthur Waley; Faber and Faber Ltd., London, for permission to include *In the Strange Isle* by Michael Roberts from COLLECTED POEMS; Longmans Green and Company Ltd., London, and New Directions Publishing Corporation, New York, for permission to include *The River God (Of the River Mimram in Hertfordshire)* by Stevie Smith from SELECTED POEMS, © 1962, 1964 by Stevie Smith; Allen and Unwin Ltd., London, and Hill and Wang, Inc., New York, for permission to include *The Beast* by Brian Patten from LITTLE JOHNNY'S CONFESSIONS; the author, Fleur Adcock, for permission to include her poem *A Game*.